THE
LIE

HEATHER DAWN GRAY

Cover photo/layout credits to Romi
Burianova and Stephen Ewashko

ISBN: 978-1-9991202-1-4

https://heatherdawngray.com/

DEDICATION

To my husband Ron, who supports women's rights, and endures sideways glances when people wonder if he is the husband found on these pages. I can assure you he is not.

And to my daughters Colby and Sabra who are strong women making a difference in this world.

ACKNOWLEDGMENTS

Being an introvert, I thought writing a novel would be perfect, how much more solitary could a profession get?

Others quickly taught me if I shared, they would help make my story better. Thank you to everyone who took the time to read my drafts and gently encouraged me to improve. Of particular mention, and in no particular order, my indebted gratitude goes to David, Allana, Debbie, Mike, Anita, Nick, Colby, Ron, Christine, Lenore, Glen, Frank, Peter, Gary, and countless others.

Thanks to Romi Burianova, Stephen Ewashko, and Sofia Abramian for the professional cover. Sofia, you captured Jahana perfectly, Romi you captured Sofia beautifully, and Stephen you put it all together magnificently.

To Colby and Sabra, thank you for always encouraging me to become better versions of myself.

Ron, I couldn't ask for better support. You ensure that while I write, we can eat. You lift me up when I'm down, steady me when I stumble, and applaud me when I soar. You are my everything.

CHAPTER ONE

A tingle of fear brushed the back of Jahana's neck. She stepped out of her office, glancing from side to side as she scooted down the hall to the coffee room. *What if another office door opens and I'm pulled inside?* Her steps quickened. The unmistakable sound of a chair scraping across the floor halted her. Silence.

"Hello?" Jahana's heart pounded in her ears, breath coming in quick bursts. Had she even spoken out loud?

Jay's head popped around the corner of the coffee room door. "Hey Jahana, you're here late."

Jahana's hand rose to her throat and she inhaled sharply. "You nearly scared me half to death." She exhaled and leaned against the wall for support.

Jay chuckled. "Sorry about that. I thought I'd start cleaning in here tonight. Looks like you had a bit of a party today."

"Yeah, it was Darren's fiftieth birthday so we had a celebration for him. I was coming down to see if there's anything left over from the potluck. Marking essays is taking longer than I thought. I swear I don't know what I was thinking when I decided to replace a multiple-choice exam with an essay." Jahana entered the coffee room and opened the fridge.

"What're you teaching?" Jay leaned on the mop, clearly happy for the diversion and company.

"Feminism in the 21st Century." Jahana spied a tub of hummus and pulled it off the top shelf as her phone dinged, causing her to jump back and lose grip on the container.

"Ahh!" She expected the lid to fly off, but it held tight.

"Trying to create more work for me?"

Jahana glanced up and Jay grinned at her.

"Yeah, sorry about that. Glad it didn't explode." Her voice trailed off as she pulled out her phone, expecting to see a message from Barid asking when she'd be home. But it was an email from the DNA testing company.

"Good news Jay! My DNA test results are in."

Jay picked up the tub of hummus and handed it to Jahana, closing the fridge door with his foot. "You mentioned getting tested when I was working days way back in January. I assumed you'd have heard by now." He reached across the counter, grabbed a box of crackers from behind some dirty dishes and handed it to Jahana.

"I knew there were some crackers here somewhere." Jahana smiled at Jay, tucking her phone back in her pocket. "No, it takes at least seven weeks to get the results back. Actually, I think they might be a few days early." Jahana raised the box of crackers at Jay and turned towards the door to the hall. "Thanks!"

"Sure anytime. I hope you find a long lost relative!"

"Me too!" Jahana shouted back as she scooted down the hall, empty rooms no longer a concern. She settled in quickly at her desk and logged into her personal email on her computer. An event like this deserved a big screen.

As she waited for the screen to load, she cracked the lid on the hummus. That's when it hit her. She closed her eyes unable to exhale. A ball of grief stuck in her throat before successively larger pieces broke off sliding into the pit of her stomach and branching out into tingles crawling down her legs. If she were standing her knees would buckle. She'd only lifted the Tupperware lid, hadn't even fully opened the container when the smell triggered her. What was in this homemade hummus that brought her maman to life?

Overwhelming sadness filled her empty spaces. The occurrence of sudden bouts of grief overwhelmed her at the most unexpected times. It could be the look in someone's eye or, like this time, the smell of something familiar. She never saw it coming and its force hit her head on.

She closed her eyes and inhaled deeply, holding her breath until she felt her lungs would burst, then exhaling forcefully to make room for gulps of new air. Oh, how she missed her maman.

A distant click of a door closing wafted down the hall. Jay must have moved on.

Jahana stared at the container in front of her before dipping a cracker in the tub, and wiping away a lone tear with the back of her hand. The screen still hadn't loaded and her mind drifted to her maman, the reason for testing her DNA.

Her maman never talked about her relatives. They were a shadow hinting at a secret life, unacknowledged. The way she brushed them off, as if none of them mattered, gnawed at Jahana. They mattered. And yet with a simple toss of her hand and a cluck of her tongue she waved them away, apparitions rendering her family's existence insignificant. That insignificance created the pebble of discontent that existed even when Jahana didn't think about it. An irritation always sitting in the pit of her stomach, an annoyance leading her to a place of no return.

Her maman's final words intruded on her thoughts, especially when grief overcame her, belying who her mother believed her to be. *You can survive this. You don't need me. You are strong.*

But Jahana didn't agree. She didn't feel as strong as her maman who battled disease with dignity. Her final words were what Jahana needed to hear. But they haunted her on the days her world crumbled and she argued with her maman like she had as a teenager. *No, I can't. Yes, I do. No, I'm not.*

At these times grief gripped her heart and made her want to curl up in the fetal position. Perhaps an appropriate response to the death of the woman who gave her life. But when the heartache receded Jahana acknowledged her maman was right. She could survive.

And Barid's gift was meant to help her move on. Not only had he remembered their anniversary, but it was a thoughtful gift. A tool to help her move on. But Jahana knew it was also a way for him to convey his allotted time for her grieving had passed. He was impatient with her grief and probably thought this was a way to get her to move on. A DNA kit to help her find her maman's family. Give her something to hang on to. Although her mind tucked pieces of her maman in a safe corner, she felt like she lost her one thought, one memory at a time. If only she knew relatives. If only she had pressed her when she was alive to talk about family.

The computer screen sprang to life and her focus returned to her DNA results. Puzzling, unexpected results. A burst of laughter escaped before she clamped her hand over her mouth, dropping the cracker, hummus pasting it to a worn tile. A gasp lodged in her windpipe; her throat narrowed. Her abdomen clenched. She scanned the page and then started again at the top. It had to be a mistake. It didn't make any sense. She pushed back her chair and rose on shaking knees. She needed fresh air, but the window wasn't the kind that opened. The frigid pane of glass felt soothing against her cheek, it grounded her. She closed her eyes hoping time would stand still or better yet, reverse. Her breath returned in spurts, heart pounding. This couldn't be happening. She focused on the rise and fall of her chest, breathing in through her nose, out through her mouth.

Disbelief and fear consumed her. How would she tell Barid? Her mind couldn't process his reaction. And then there was her father. Did he already know? He had insisted she not take the test. Was this why? He seemed baffled by her belief that science could show her who she was. And yet it told her something he never had.

Her baba's words intruded on her thoughts. *Do you doubt who you are? Why do you have to ask someone else where you come from? You are Jahana. Only living child of Emad and Noosha. A Seyyed, direct descendent of Muhammad. A survivor. Brought into this world to spread joy amid great loss. Your maman and I celebrated you while burying your twin. And we have loved you from the moment of creation. What will science tell you that you don't already know?*

She tried to explain the feeling in the pit of her stomach. The need to find her maman's relatives. But his anger prevented him from hearing. He never mentioned the testing again. Jahana knew he believed if he didn't mention it, it would go away.

She wished she had listened to him. But it was too late. Nothing made sense.

Her breathing normalized, and she fell back into her office chair, pushing aside the crackers and hummus. She massaged her temples as she read and reread the DNA test details. Finally, she took a deep breath, logged out of her account, and placed the student's work in front of her. Her mind kept wandering to Barid and what he would say. What he would do. She rubbed the back of her neck and with all the concentration she could muster, marked the last essay.

When she looked up, the office clock indicated it was later than the two previous nights. She added the paper to the pile of completed marking, rose and reached into her office drawer for her purse. She didn't bother to grab her briefcase; she'd be back in less than nine hours. She slung her purse over her shoulder, grabbed the office keys and glanced at the many piles of papers on her desk. The cracker face-down on the floor, caught her eye, but she didn't have the energy to pick it up, instead she took a deep breath and closed her office door.

Her heels echoed in the empty stairwell as she descended into the underground parkade. The door above closed slowly, but loudly, causing her pace to quicken. Exiting the stairwell, she held her car key in her fist so it extended between her fingers, a self-defense move she'd learned in a class years ago. She kept her head up, looking from one side to the other. The clip of her heels resonated in the mostly empty parkade. A lone van parked behind her car. She craned her neck to look around her vehicle before approaching and quickly climbing in, pulling the door closed behind her and locking it. A sigh escaped her lips as she looked in the rear-view mirror. No movement whatsoever. Her car roared to life and she drove up the ramp and into the night. A cat ran across the street in front of her as she turned onto Nicholas Street, and left Ottawa's downtown core.

She pulled into her driveway. How many red lights had she run? The last thing she remembered was a figure emerging from the shadows, skate blades catching motorists' headlights as he glided along the canal near the freeway onramp.

She slid the gear shift into park and turned the key. A last wisp of exhaust floated past the passenger window, rising through the crisp winter air. She rested her chin on the steering wheel and stared up at the darkened windows. At least she wouldn't have to face Barid tonight. She leaned back and closed her eyes, paralyzed by the evening's events.

Jahana took a deep breath and exhaled slowly, the cold bringing her back to reality. If the neighbours noticed they'd wonder what she was doing sitting in her vehicle so late at night. Inside the house, she leaned on the door and slid the deadbolt into place before hanging up her jacket in the entryway closet. She crept down the hall and through the kitchen, not bothering to turn on any lights; she knew this house intimately. Her hand lingered on the old milk door above the ledge at the back entrance before she descended the stairs to the basement. She grew up here. After she and Barid married, her parents moved into a smaller place and allowed them to rent to own. Jahana loved this house and wouldn't want to raise her girls anywhere else.

In her study she stared again at the results on her laptop screen. Would this outcome take everything from her? The girls were still too young to understand how it might affect their relationship with their baba. Her stomach turned thinking about Cyra and Sahba. She was strong enough to handle the fallout, but the collateral damage reached much farther than her.

Her body suddenly felt heavy and she shut down the computer, plodding up both sets of stairs. She avoided eye contact with herself as she released the pin under her chin and removed the hijab in the ensuite mirror. Her fingers lingered on the soft chiffon cloth as she folded it, leaving it on the counter instead of hanging it in the closet with the others, not wanting to wake Barid.

She quietly removed her blouse and pants, laying them on the trunk at the end of the bed, and slipped into her pajamas. As she pulled back the covers, a voice pierced the darkness.

"Welcome home."

She froze.

"Thank you," she whispered as she climbed into bed, hoping Barid would leave it at that and fall asleep.

"Did you hear about the bombing in Palestine?"

Jahana raised her head. "No! Is your family okay?"

"Yes, it appears so" Barid rolled from his back to his side, and faced her.

"Oh, I'm so sorry. You must have been worried sick." Jahana settled her head on the pillow, keeping her eyes on Barid.

"Maman called and let me know they're okay." He paused before continuing. "Of course, the Canadian and American governments have not denounced the Jews for the bombs. I'm so sick of the Jews getting away with murder."

Jahana remained silent, but reached over and rubbed his hand.

He suddenly pulled away as if her touch repelled him. "Another late night. Did you get the marking finished?" His words rang sharp, crisp, unexpected.

Her eyes adjusted to the darkness and the details in Barid's face came into focus. His jaw muscles twitched as the almost imperceptible sound of grinding teeth fell between them.

"Yes. I'm all done. I'm not sure if I'll continue with this assessment next year." She pulled the covers up around her ears and shuddered.

"I would suggest you don't. The girls have missed you at dinner. And I'm sick of warming up meals for us. Your number one responsibility is here. Don't forget that."

"Of course. I promise I'll be home on time tomorrow."

"Good." He rolled over, ending the inquisition.

Jahana breathed a slow measured sigh of relief. Again, she was alone with the secret. Irrational thoughts of Barid's reaction to her DNA results weighed on her, but heavy eyelids meant sleep would overcome her quickly. Tomorrow she'd figure out how to deal with her Jewish ancestry.

CHAPTER TWO

The sun warmed her face. She pulled the covers over her head. But something bothered her, sitting at the back of her mind, niggling her awake. *Sun? What day is it? Did I sleep in?* Her hand escaped the covers and fanned the top of the nightstand until she located her phone and pulled it close. She opened one eye long enough to see the time. *Damn. Why didn't Barid wake me?* His angry voice from the night before seeped into her memory. *Guess he showed me.*

Swinging her legs over the side of the bed, she groaned before stumbling to the shower. The water warmed quickly, and she stepped in. That's when the reality of her DNA results struck full force. Was it a nightmare? But the pit of her stomach reminded her otherwise. There was no time to languish in the stream of hot water. She was going to be late.

The echo of Barid closing the front door greeted her as her feet nestled into the soft pile of the bathmat. Then the girls' voices rose from their bathroom.

"Is that my hairbrush you're using?"

"Yeah, but I can't find mine."

"You could've at least asked before taking it, Sahba. You drive me crazy!"

Cyra's bedroom door slammed shut. Jahana wondered how her two daughters were so different. *Couldn't one morning be free of arguments*? But she consoled herself with the fact she wouldn't have to coax them out of bed.

She glanced at the clock and realized she was making up lost time. As she set out the cereal bowls, Sahba wandered into the kitchen. A frown on her face vanished when she saw Jahana.

"Maman! I missed you last night." She ran to her, grabbing her around the waist and holding tight.

Jahana held her, grateful for the rare opportunity to hug her daughter who hated hugs.

"Oh Sahba. I missed you too and I'm sorry for the late nights this week. I promise I'll be home on time this afternoon. Cereal's on the table and your lunch is in the fridge."

Sahba let go and perched herself on the bar stool at the island. Jahana tousled her hair as she exited the kitchen. She peered up the stairs from the entryway, but Cyra's door remained closed.

"Cyra, I'm leaving for work. Please make sure you and your sister aren't late for the bus. I'll see you after school."

There was a pause before Cyra replied. "Okay, Maman."

Jahana hoped Cyra wouldn't bring the exasperation she heard in her voice downstairs, but she knew the hairbrush would likely still be a topic of discussion at dinner. The door closed behind her and she ducked into the car. The LED clock indicated she might make it on time if traffic wasn't too heavy. Maybe the sleep-in was for the best; she avoided Barid and bought herself time.

****

The smell of hummus permeated her nostrils as she unlocked the door, and grief again gripped her. The tub lay open on her desk from the previous night. *What a waste.* She snapped the lid on, scraped the cracker off the floor and threw both into the hall trash, returning the cracker box to the coffee room. She closed the door and paused to centre herself before retreating behind her desk, not wanting to chat with anyone. She needed time to think.

Before her first class Jahana entered essay marks into the computer and reviewed lecture notes for the day. She dealt with work emails, and contemplated opening her account to look at the DNA report again. Was she over-reacting?

She stared at the computer screen. A headache pulsed in her temples and she realized she was clenching her jaw.

She consciously relaxed, moving her mouth from side to side and rubbing her cheeks. *Please let the results be different.* But nothing changed.

So, what were Jewish genes anyway? Was it a hoax? How could a religion have a gene? She opened her browser and typed in her query. All kinds of hits appeared and they all seemed to have their own slant. Most seemed to think the gene was specific to Jewish populations because of how tight knit their communities were and the gene could be traced back to four women founders. Even though Judaism was a religion, there clearly was a gene attributed to some Jewish descendants. Where could her gene have come from? She was always told she was a direct descendent of Muhammad on her father's side. Did that mean her mother was Jewish? Or was the whole Seyyed thing a hoax?

She typed in another search to determine how DNA is passed from parents to children. It became clear fifty percent of each of her parents contributed DNA. For her to be identified as 50% Ashkenazi Jew, one parent had to be close to one hundred percent Ashkenazi Jew. It would be a long shot, but if her parent's each carried smaller amounts of Jewish genes, she might happen to inherit all of the them from both parents. But the chances of that happening were very slim. The more logical explanation was one parent carried predominantly Ashkenazi Jewish genes.

If one parent carried such a large percentage of Ashkenazi genetic material, they must have a direct lineage to Jewish ancestry. Why wouldn't they have told her about that? A Jew converting to Islam wasn't something her parents would have been ashamed of. Revealing a Jewish heritage might have been troublesome during the revolution in Iran when Jews were being persecuted. But why would they keep it a secret once they were safely in Canada?

Having so much Jewish ancestry made no sense. *Maybe these results are a mistake. Could my sample have been mixed up with someone else's? Could the results belong to someone else? The matches of three second and ninety-eight third and fourth cousins revealed no recognizable names. What other explanation was there? That must be it. The results aren't from my sample.*

The weight lifted from her heart. It was a mistake. But her breath caught when she thought about telling Barid. What conclusions would he draw regardless of whether the testing was correct? She could hear his antisemitic tirade at the mere mention of Jewish genes. His family still lived in Palestine and he harboured their anger. He often talked about returning one day and fighting alongside his people for what was rightfully theirs. She didn't share his views. She had a few Jewish colleagues and enjoyed their company, not that she'd ever be able to tell him that. She wished Barid could get past his upbringing and his irrational thoughts, but after twenty-five years in Canada it wasn't likely he would change.

A quick glance at the clock and Jahana rose from her chair, stashing her jump drive in her pocket and picking up the stack of marked papers before heading to the classroom. She raced down the hall, trying to figure out how she would explain the results to Barid. Just before she reached her destination, it hit her. She'd order a second DNA test kit and tell Barid the DNA testing company requested a new sample because they spoiled the first one.

The day brightened, and her stride slowed. Things would be okay.

It was afternoon before Jahana returned to her office. She rummaged through her desk drawer before finding the Visa card hidden in the back. She only used it for purchases she didn't want to explain to Barid. There was the occasion she bought Darren a thank you gift for his help with technical problems. Barid would never understand why his wife was buying another man a book online.

She used her work address on the order form and paid off the Visa with the money she squirreled away in a different bank. The ninety-nine dollars, would be hard to replace. Barid's anniversary gift was turning out to be the worst present she ever received.

An involuntary sigh escaped her lips when she pressed the 'order now' button. Even the fog that overshadowed her thoughts all day cleared. It was early, but with the extra time she put in the past few days she didn't feel guilty packing up and heading home. She looked forward to an evening with the girls to catch up on their lives, even if it included the hairbrush argument from the morning.

Students moved between classes and Jahana wove her way through the crowds to the parkade. It felt much friendlier below ground than it did the night before. She pulled onto Nicholas, the traffic heavy and slow. Her mind returned to her results and the lie she would have to tell Barid. He gave her the kit and he'd ask about the results sooner or later. She hated lying. Maybe she could put it off. Tonight, she'd make his favourite dinner and the girls would monopolize the conversation. The subject shouldn't come up. Sometime over the next couple of days she'd slip it in. She wanted to bring it up before he did, ensure the discussion was on her terms. Be more prepared to control her emotions. She didn't need to be caught on the defensive.

Besides, the repeat test would come back with different results.

****

Jahana picked Sunday to lie to Barid. *Would he see right through her?* She needed to be busy doing something else when she told him. If he saw her eyes, he'd know she was lying.

She opened the oven door and lifted the roaster out, setting it on top of the stove. Behind her back Barid unscrewed the cap from a bottle of Perrier and poured it into a tumbler. She heard the ice cubes clink as he swirled the liquid.

She glanced over her shoulder, before turning back to the roaster. "Oh, I meant to tell you. I received a message from MyGeneticFamily yesterday." Jahana paused to control her breathing and her voice. "Apparently, they messed up my sample and have asked me to resubmit. They're sending me another kit."

Jahana lifted the lid off the pan and stabbed a fork in the chicken, clear juices ran out. It was ready, but she replaced the lid, opened the oven door and set it back in, turning down the heat.

"I meant to ask if you heard from them. That's frustrating. They sound incompetent."

"I suppose they're just human." She fiddled with the temperature control on the oven, hands shaking. "At least they admitted to their mistake and didn't release inaccurate results." *Damn, why didn't I just agree with him?*

"I suppose."

Jahana turned in time to see Barid wander out of the kitchen. She breathed a sigh of relief and leaned on the counter for support. There, she'd done it. She finished preparing dinner.

****

The snow storms of March turned to rain in April. The transition of winter to spring happened quickly in Ottawa. During that time Jahana convinced herself the original DNA results were impossible. As April 18, the anniversary of her mother's death approached, Jahana's heart ached. She wanted to mark the anniversary somehow, but how? Then on the day, an email appeared in her inbox. The results of her second sample for DNA testing were available.

She was at work staring at her inbox. Unable to open her account. Unlike the first time, she dreaded clicking on the link. She'd been thinking about her maman all day. It was ironic the results appeared in her inbox on this day of all days. Was it an omen? And if it was, was it good? She wasn't sure her maman would approve of her digging up a past she'd worked hard to keep secret.

Jahana's stomach gurgled and her bowels twisted. She rose, dashing for the bathroom at the end of the hall. As she passed Darren's office, she glimpsed his head raise.

"Are you okay, Jahana?"

"Yes," she replied before ducking into the bathroom, making it just in time. Nervous bowels gave her problems, but she didn't realize the DNA results worried her this much. Clearly, she wasn't as convinced of the errors in the first results as she thought.

Time slowed, and she sat on the toilet longer than she needed, hoping Darren had a class to teach. She didn't want to run into him and have to face his concerns for her strange behavior; it was more than embarrassing. Or was she trying to delay the inevitable? Put off seeing these second DNA results?

Still, she lingered, unable to stand and confront what was waiting for her in the office. She shivered as small beads of sweat trickled along her spine.

Pull it together. This is ridiculous. Islam speaks to my heart. The results won't affect who I am.

But it wasn't true. If the results confirmed the earlier test, Barid would make sure her life and their girls' lives changed. She knew there would be no going back.

But she was getting ahead of herself, because this email was about to set everything straight, and later this evening she would share her results with Barid.

Standing and exiting the stall, she looked at herself in the mirror, willing courage into her terrified image. She walked back to her office, letting out a whisper of relief when she passed Darren's closed door. She hesitated before walking to her chair, taking a seat, positioning the cursor, and clicking on the email.

The repeat DNA test will confirm I don't have Jewish descent. She swallowed hard. Her bowels complained again. The full reality of her genetic makeup popped up on the computer and glared back at her. She touched the screen, hoping that it wasn't real. But there it was - 49% Caucasus, 48% Ashkenazi Jew and other insignificant traces.

Jew. *I'm Jewish?* Born in Iran to Muslim parents, there was no chance half of her DNA carried Ashkenazi Jewish traits. That meant at least one of her parents was Jewish. *Impossible.* There would be no reason for them not to tell her. Being a converted Jew wasn't something Muslims hid. There was no shame in it.

Yet, Barid would be very ashamed and angry. She could lie to him, but would that be fair to the girls? Could she do to them what had been done to her? Allow them to think they were something they weren't? With the prevalence of DNA testing chances are they would find out some day. They had a right to know who they were. There was nothing to be ashamed of. She didn't want them getting into a relationship where having Jewish genes was a problem. Barid never would have married her if he knew she had Jewish ancestry. If she had known before she was married, she could have avoided being in a marriage with someone who wouldn't tolerate her Jewish genes. He would never have dated her to begin with. But because her Jewish ancestry had been kept secret, her genes could have major impacts on their relationship. And his relationship with their children.

Jahana wasn't sure how long the screen glowed in front of her before she started a new email informing her supervisor and colleagues she wasn't feeling well and leaving for the day.

****

"Anyone home?" She called out as she entered the house, but in the early afternoon she knew there wouldn't be an answer.

20

Silence echoed. As she climbed the stairs, she unwound her hijab, letting it fall to the floor when she entered her bedroom. Her pulse throbbed in the back of her neck. She collapsed on the bed and hung her head over the edge to ease the migraine edging up from the base of her skull. Through closed eyes she prayed for guidance. How would she tell Barid? Her baba? Her girls? Tears pooled and fell to the beige rug.

Before she married him, she wouldn't have had trouble telling Barid about her results. While many Muslims might still consider him a liberal, his conservative ways became apparent after the wedding. He used to like her zest for life and belief in gender equality. But once they uttered the wedding vows, he assumed the role of patriarch. Combine his ideals with his antisemitic upbringing and she knew she couldn't tell him the results.

Jahana's eyes closed, and she sighed. Her thoughts stabilized. Mishal would know what to do. Her eyes snapped open. This could affect Mishal too. They were cousins, their fathers were brothers. *What if Jewish blood runs through her veins too?* There was more to consider than how the results affected herself. And if it was her mother that was Jewish, and it didn't affect Mishal, how could she ask her to keep a secret like that? She'd have to think about this longer. It wasn't something she could just blurt out to Mishal.

The migraine abated, allowing her to roll over and stand. She stumbled into the bathroom. Barid's aftershave lingered causing her intestines to clench again at the thought of telling him her secret. The coolness of the washcloth soothed her puffy eyes, and she stood in silence willing her day to normalcy. Screeching bus brakes commanded her return to reality, prompting her to take a deep breath and look at her reflection. The key turned in the front door. She took another slow breath, determined to return herself to normal. Pre-DNA test normal.

Cyra's voice sang out, "Maman are you home?"

"Yes, I'm upstairs. I'll be right down."

Jahana stood at the top of the stairs watching her girls remove their shoes. Cyra hung up her hijab then, grabbed her sister's lunch bag and skipped out of sight into the kitchen. Sahba trailed less enthusiastically.

Jahana inhaled and descended the stairs, putting the results on simmer. When she allowed things to percolate, she found a way forward. This was no different. Right now, she would pretend nothing had changed.

She entered the kitchen, and embraced the girls more tightly than usual, Sahba wiggled out from under her arm. They were her world. For them she would do anything.

In that moment Jahana recognized the need to trace her DNA; figure out how Ashkenazi Jew featured in her genes. The DNA reached farther than the skin that defined her. There were implications for her girls and it was up to her to make sure Cyra and Sahba knew their ancestry. She would find the origin of her Jewish genes before she revealed the results to anyone.

****

Barid wasn't home to put his arm around her, to tell her how much her maman would be proud of her or to sit in silence as she remembered her on this one-year anniversary of her death. He had forgotten. But she had her girls.

"Cyra and Sahba, come with me to the bedroom, I have something to show you." Jahana needed them to remember. Not just the day her life ended, but how wonderful she was. What a strong woman she was. And how much she loved them all.

"It was a year ago today that Mamani passed away." Jahana took the wooden box off the shelf of her closet and blew the dust off the top.

"I remembered." Cyra sighed.

"You did? Why didn't you say anything?" Jahana set the box on the bed and put her arm around Cyra.

"I didn't want to make you sad." Cyra peered up at Jahana through long eyelashes.

"That doesn't make me sad, it makes me happy. I'm glad you remember."

"I'm sorry I didn't remember, Maman." Sahba studied her feet, her fingers twisting the bottom of her T-shirt.

"Girls, girls it's all okay." Jahana placed her other arm around Sahba's shoulders. After a quick squeeze she picked up the box and sat on the edge of the bed. "Come sit beside me. Now, before I open this box, Sahba, tell me something you remember about Mamani?"

Sahba tugged at the corner of her lip with her finger before her eyes brightened. "Her doughnuts. How she would come over and make doughnuts all day and then that's what we'd eat for dinner."

"Oh, that's a great memory. Her doughnuts were the very best, the thought makes my mouth water. What about you Cyra, what do you remember?"

Cyra turned to her with a big grin. "Remember when she used to hold up knitting to her chin and say, 'what do you think, am I almost done?'." Cyra giggled. "And she'd do it even if she only had a couple of rows done." Cyra burst into laughter and Jahana and Sahba joined her.

It felt good to laugh.

"What about you Maman? What do you remember?" Cyra put her head on Jahana's shoulder, her laughter replaced by a shudder.

"Oh, so much, but I guess I have to say the time she sewed my wedding dress. She spent months hand-stitching it. Her finger-tips bled from pushing on the end of the needle. It was a labour of love. And I felt so special wearing it."

"Do you still have it? Can we see it?" Sahba jumped off the bed in anticipation.

"Oh, it's packed away, but yes I still have it in case either one of you want to wear it when you get married."

"Dibs!" Both girls chimed at the same time.

"No reason you both can't wear it if you want to. Now sit back up beside me, I want to show you something. I put a few special things from Maman inside this memory box. I haven't looked at it since she died and really can't remember what's inside."

Jahana carefully raised the lid to reveal an assortment of papers and odds and ends. The girls peered inside.

"What's that." Cyra pointed to a broach in the shape of the letter J.

"That's a broach my maman gave me when I was about your age. It came from her maman's family. What do you think the 'J' is for?"

"Jahana!" Both girls shouted at once.

"Wrong!" Jahana shouted back.

"What do you mean wrong? What's it stand for then?" Cyra picked the broach up and turned it over.

"It stands for Jahakhana. My maman's maiden name. It's the name she used when trying to figure out what to call me."

"Cool. Can I see it?"

Cyra handed it to Sahba who held it up to her collar bone. "Are those real diamonds?"

"No, if they were, I wouldn't be keeping it in here. It would be worth a fortune. They're just rhinestones."

Sahba placed the broach back in the box and took out a piece of paper, handing it to Jahana to unfold.

"This is Maman and Baba's marriage certificate. See it's in Persian." Jahana ran her fingers across the faded ink lettering before refolding it.

"Is that a book?" Cyra pointed to a yellowed cover with grey bird silhouettes peeking out from under other papers.

"Yes, I'd forgotten that was in here. It's a very special book." Jahana moved the papers aside and lifted it from the bottom of the box. Her hand lingered on the cover and she took a deep breath.

"When Maman passed away, her hand rested on this book. It lay on her chest face down like she had just finished reading it."

25

"Had she?" Sahba's eyes grew large. "Did she die while reading it?"

Jahana smiled. "No sweetheart. She wasn't able to read the last few days, but I knew she loved the book. I don't know if she could hear me or not, but I read her passages from it those last few days. I put it on her chest and rested her hand on it as I held her hand in mine. It seemed to bring her peace."

Sahba and Cyra sat in silence.

"It was a book she read to me many times as I grew up. It's a complex book and the first time she read it I didn't understand. But she explained a little more every time. Eventually I read it by myself and still learned new things."

"Can you read it to us?" Sahba reached out to feel the worn cover.

"I'd like that. And Maman would too."

"What's it about?" Cyra seemed a little less enthused about the prospect of being read to by her mother.

"Well, it's a story that comes from the Quran and told in a very long poem. In fact, the entire book is one poem."

Cyra rolled her eyes. "Do we have to read it?"

"I know I'm not making it sound very good, but it really is. How about we read a little bit every now and then? I won't take away from your reading time every night. The story symbolizes the choices people make to either remain unchanged or become liberated."

"What's liberated?" Sahba continued to run her finger over the cover.

"It means smarter, able to see other people's points of view. The story talks about seven valleys people navigate

26

many times in their lives. The first valley is the Quest followed by Love, Understanding, Independence and Detachment, Unity, Astonishment and Bewilderment, and finally Deprivation and Death. I really do think you'll like it if you give it a try. I know Maman would be so happy to know I'm introducing the two of you to it."

"Okay. But do we have to do it tonight?" Cyra squinted up at her.

"No, not tonight." Jahana rose and placed the box on the bed. "Tell you what. You and Sahba look through the jewelry in the bottom of the box and I'll go get a couple of Ziploc bags. I'll put your names on the bags. You can pick one thing out of the box that you would like someday and I'll put it in your bag. Every year on April 18, we'll do this."

The girls dove into the box and Jahana retreated to the kitchen. Her heart felt lighter. It was good to remember, to keep her maman's memory alive. And she looked forward to reading the book to the girls. She couldn't help but feel Noosha watched over them.

CHAPTER THREE

“**C**an I go to a movie with Souri on Saturday?” Cyra glanced at Barid and turned to stare at Jahana before dropping her gaze. She pushed peas around on her plate.

Jahana glanced across the table at Barid. He stared at his plate and lifted a forkful to his mouth, chewing slowly. She wished she could predict his response. Jahana put down her fork and waited.

“Hey Jahana, did you get those DNA results back yet?” Barid raised his eyes, staring at her, ignoring Cyra.

Jahana lowered her gaze. Her hands shook, and she rested them in her lap while she contemplated her response.

Over two weeks passed since she received the repeat results and she avoided telling Barid. She meant to, but never worked up the nerve. And when the topic didn't come up, she hoped he'd forgotten. She lived in an unrealistic world, carrying on as if it never happened.

But the dreaded moment hung in the air. All eyes settled on her. Even the girls stopped eating and turned their attention her way. Cyra fidgeted, knowing her question might never get answered, in which case she wouldn't be going. Jahana considered bringing the conversation back to Cyra, but that wouldn't help her cause or Cyra's. The scenarios she prepared on the off chance he asked about her DNA, played out in her mind.

She wanted to take a deep breath, but stopped herself. Barid continued to stare at her. How she responded might be more important than what she said. Barid saw through lies, but perhaps she didn't have to tell the entire story. She'd be vague without appearing to be hiding something.

Remain calm, this has to come off nonchalant. She didn't want to say something she'd regret. Barid's sixth sense caught the slightest flaws. This would be hard to get past him.

"Oh, yes, I did. I meant to tell you. They disappointed me, not much information at all. The test revealed cousins whose names I don't recognize."

"But isn't that what you hoped for? You did this to find unknown relatives, and it sounds like that's what you found?"

She took a shallow breath and forced her muscles to relax, pasting a slight smile on her face before responding. "It's just that I didn't recognize even one last name. I would have expected Jahakhana to show up somewhere. I'll follow up. Work's been busy and I've been trying to catch up around here too. It makes me question the validity of the test after they contaminated the first sample."

"How do you contact them, through email?"

Barid wanted to have this conversation. The girls stared at the table, no longer interested in their food. They didn't dare interrupt.

"No, a message app within the MyGeneticFamily website allows me to contact any matches. But the relationships are distant cousins. Another reason I'm not sure about pursuing this."

"Sahba!" Milk shot across the table into Barid's lap. He leaped to his feet, shaking a finger at her. "You need to be more careful. Ask someone to pass the bowl rather than reach!" Barid pounded the table before he stomped out of the room.

The distraction gave Jahana the break in conversation she needed. She rushed to the kitchen for towels and tissues.

Sahba sobbed. "I'm sorry Maman." She caught Cyra's eye before she rose from the table. "I'm sorry to you too, Cyra."

"Not your fault." Cyra mumbled and started clearing the table.

"It's okay. An accident, just a little milk that's all." The towels soaked up the mess, and she gave Sahba a hug. The tears subsided as the TV roared to life in the living room. The inquisition forgotten, at least for the moment.

The girls finished removing the dishes from the table and Jahana shooed them out of the kitchen. Cyra called Souri to tell her the bad news and withdrew to her room. Sahba disappeared downstairs, the TV blared from below. Jahana stomped twice, and the volume quietened. She rinsed the dishes and loaded the dishwasher all the while thinking about her plan. Even though she'd bought a little time, Barid's unpredictability meant a conversation might start up again. She needed to be prepared. *First step, talk to Baba without raising his suspicions.* Jahana stared out the window above the sink and sighed.

****

The phone rang several times before Jahana heard a connection followed by a pause before a husky voice answered.

"Hey Baba, good morning. How are you?"

Emad coughed. Jahana glanced at the clock. It was ten thirty but his voice carried the jagged edge of someone who just woke up.

"Jahana, what a pleasant surprise." Emad coughed again. "I'm well and hope you are too. How are my favourite grandchildren?"

"Easy to call them favourite when they're your only grandchildren, Baba."

The familiar chuckle rattled over the phone. A welcome sound, even if forced. At least he tried.

"I wondered if you'd like to meet me for lunch tomorrow? I've been busy, but things have let up and I want to see you, even if it's over lunch at work. What do you say?"

"That would be nice."

The dullness in his voice worried Jahana. Her maman's death affected him and he didn't seem to be moving forward like he needed to. How do you help someone do that? *I need to include him more.*

"Oh good, I'm glad you can come. Does 11:30, at my office, work for you?" She sighed. Noosha was the love of his life.

"Works perfectly."

She hung up the phone and sat staring at it. He struggled to move on. Her maman's memory hung over both their lives. When she accepted Barid's marriage proposal she considered Barid the love of her life too. But within the first year of marriage, he changed. When Cyra arrived, he assumed she would quit university, but she used the hijab as a bargaining chip. He pushed her to wear it shortly after she married, but she resisted. But there were hills to die on, and wearing the hijab wasn't one of them. If she could stay in school, it was worth the trade-off. When Sahba was born, the fight started again. Six months after Sahba's birth she applied for a professorship at the university and received a job offer. Barid yelled and insisted she stay home, but she convinced him having a wife as a university professor looked favourably on him. By this point any thoughts of spending her life with a soulmate vanished.

Barid declared her outside activities needed to allow her to continue to carry out duties as a wife and mother. When her job became overwhelming, he reminded her of her priorities. Some days she wondered why she continued to fight, but her maman taught her to value education. Women's education was a privilege denied many, making it important for her to stand up for her rights in Canada. The day Jahana graduated with a PhD her maman wept with pride.

"Through education women will gain equality." Noosha's words echoed in her head every single day. Strong, meaningful words that Jahana instilled in her girls too. And now she would also teach them about their ancestry. Why hadn't her maman seen the significance in that?

Would she understand my need to find her ancestors? To find out why I have Jewish blood? Why didn't you tell me before you died? Did you know?

Jahana shook her head back to the present. This talk with her baba needed to be a good first step in solving the mystery.

CHAPTER FOUR

Mishal furrowed her brows. *What's going on with you?* They rarely missed their weekly coffee date and Jahana blew her off for the third week in a row. It caused an unsettled feeling. A tingle ran up her spine. Something wasn't right.

She grabbed a T-shirt from the laundry beside her on the couch, looked down at the folded clothes on the coffee table and realized she mixed up the boys' piles. She leaned back and rested her head on the couch.

We've never gone this long without meeting up. Even your texts seem short and abrupt. But maybe it's my imagination. You're likely busy finishing up the school year.

But her gut told her otherwise. Jahana avoided her for a reason and it was more than just being busy. It brought back memories of the hijab. When Jahana faced her after two weeks of avoidance she was shocked to see her wearing the hijab. As a teenager Mishal remembered Jahana commenting on the piece of cloth being a sign of women's oppression. While she knew she had outgrown those views and learned to accept that wearing it could be an individual's choice, Mishal had a hard time believing Jahana had changed her mind about not being a woman who wore it. Although she hesitated to say Jahana was oppressed, she had a hard time believing she had changed her mind about wearing the hijab without Barid's influence.

Jahana's absence in her life was not a good sign.

Mishal leaned forward, re-sorted the piles and continued to fold. A soccer tournament meant a busy weekend ahead. She looked forward to watching the boys play, and she loved that Hamid was coaching them this year.

School would be out soon. Another reason to meet up with Jahana. The summer break would take away their coffee opportunity.

I'll invite Jahana, Barid and the girls to one game on the weekend. Barid never came to anything she invited him to, but she continued to include him. She grabbed her phone off the end table and sent off a text to Jahana asking them to come to a game on Saturday and then stop by for a barbecue. The reply came back immediately.

Sorry we have other plans.

This time of year was busy for everyone, but Mishal couldn't help feel there was more to it. *I wonder if Uncle Emad knows what's going on?*

Before she could talk herself out of it, she punched out his number. The phone continued to ring, and she wondered if she should bother him. Just when she was about to hang up, he answered.

"Uncle Emad, it's Mishal. How are you?" Voices peppered the background. "I'm sorry do you have company?"

"No, no, dear. I'm at the bus stop headed to the university to meet Jahana for lunch. So nice of you to call." Emad's voice smiled, and Mishal was relieved to hear it. He'd been sad for so long.

"Oh, I won't keep you. I was checking in to see how you're doing. I've worried about Jahana. She's been so busy, but I'm glad you're meeting up with her." Mishal's heart lifted. Jahana was juggling work and her family and her baba. *I need to stop obsessing about this, it's not always about me.*

She hung up the phone and pulled out the vacuum cleaner, starting in her bedroom and making her way into the boys' room, working quickly. This new cordless vacuum barely had enough power to get both floors done before the battery died. As she reached under the bunk-bed, the suction squealed. Mishal flipped over the nozzle and worked a corner of paper free without tearing.

The paper was folded with Adar's name printed on the front. A word in capital letters scrawled in red ink bled through the paper. The word caused her heart to race, and she unfolded it. *TERRORIST* stared back at her. He'd been quiet lately, but she assumed worries about summer caused his mood. He liked structure in his life and he liked school.

Her heart sank as she thought about what he must be going through. Why hadn't he said anything?

She worked her jaw back and forth as she tucked the note in her pocket. Jahana dealt with this kind of bullying with her girls. She'd know what to do.

She set the vacuum back on the charger and texted Jahana.

> *Call when you get a chance. Adar's being bullied and I need your advice.*

The phone rang and Mishal answered on the first ring.

"Oh, Mishal I'm so sorry about Adar. What's happened?"

Mishal explained the note. "What should I do?"

"Oh, I wish I had better advice, but other than moving the boys to a Muslim school, I have little for you. When the girls were bullied, I don't think we handled it well. Instead of trying to educate and deal with the situation, we fled. It's hard to take a stand when your child's safety is at risk."

Mishal could hear the concern in Jahana's voice.

"Hamid and I agreed we wanted to keep the boys in public school, but now I'm not sure that was the best thing for them. But I'm not ready to move them yet. Not that

I'm saying what you did was wrong." Mishal hoped she wasn't coming across judgmental. Jahana had Barid to deal with. She didn't have a choice in how they responded to the girls' situation.

There was a pause on the line before Jahana responded. "Would calling the principal be a good first step?"

"Maybe. Might as well start at the top. Mr. Clarke seems like a reasonable man. Sorry to bother you with all of this, but you're always my first call when I need someone to talk things through. Miss you, cousin."

"Oh Mishal, I've been so self-absorbed. I'm sorry I've cancelled our coffee dates. Let's get together next Friday. What do you say?"

Mishal stopped pacing. "Coffee next Friday sounds great, but why've you been self-absorbed? That isn't like you at all? What's wrong?"

"Oh, I, I, ah…I've just been so busy at work with year-end. I haven't had time to lift my head and look around me. That's all. Please call anytime you need to talk about Adar or anything. I'm never too busy for you. I mean, I have been, but not anymore."

"Nice talking to you. No worries, cousin. See you next Friday." Mishal stared at the phone after pressing the button to disconnect. Jahana didn't usually stumble over words.

****

Emad peered down the street and tapped his foot, checking his watch again. It had been a long time since he rode the bus, but a parking spot would cost almost as much as his lunch. Perhaps saving money wasn't worth the wait. He rose to walk back home when the number four bus turned the corner and whined to a halt. The door opened and Emad grasped the handrail to pull himself up the three stairs to the coin box. *When did I become so weak and tired?*

"Hello Emad. It's been awhile."

Emad had his coins ready to deposit but the bus driver covered the coin deposit. "This one's on me," he whispered as he winked and nodded his head for Emad to sit down up front.

"Bob you've changed buses. No longer on the hospital route?" Emad smiled graciously before settling into his seat.

"Nah, they changed things up when the new train line started running. I liked my old route, but I'm grateful not to be one of the drivers let go. And I'm getting used to the new streets and stops."

Emad fidgeted on the bench seat just behind and across from Bob. The emptiness of the spot beside him a hollow reminder of all he lost. Like so many things, the seat, the bus, Bob, gave him the feeling many would call wistful. But it wasn't wistful at all. It was raw and painful and his eyes welled up. He glanced at Bob. Thankfully he was watching the road. He turned his head to the window behind him to wipe away the tears sliding down his cheeks. His sagging gray reflection startled him.

The bus glided to another stop, and he took a deep breath and turned back around. He heard the baby's cries before the bus door opened, and a mother maneuvered a stroller on board settling in across from him. Emad smiled. He wished he could tell her it was going to be okay. Even though she probably thought this phase would never end, it would. And one day she would wish she had it back. But he didn't say anything. It was pointless. She wouldn't understand until she too lived through the phases, realizing too late, she should have embraced them instead of wishing them away.

The bus filled to capacity as it neared the university. A young man with headphones sat next to Emad, in Noosha's seat. A flood of guilt and remorse washed over him as the smoke of this stranger's last cigarette clung to his leather jacket and permeated Emad's world. *What an awful, wonderful scent.* It brought back Noosha and the guilt for not encouraging her to quit. He closed his eyes and pretended she was beside him, not an insolent twenty-something. There were so many things he would tell her. He would convince her smoking was no way to give the finger to Iran's oppressive regime. It was not liberating, like she believed it to be. He would slide his arm across the back of the seat and give her a squeeze. And she would turn to him in surprise, as he so rarely showed affection in public. He would say he loved her and never wanted to live without her.

The bus turned a corner and the boy who was not Noosha, leaned into him, interrupting Emad's thoughts and snapping his eyes open. His stop loomed ahead.

"Talk to you later," he mumbled to Noosha as the last wisp of her settled into the back of his mind. Someone pulled the cord and the 'stopping' sign flashed above his head.

He patted Bob's shoulder as he exited the bus.

"Thanks again Bob. Have a good day."

"You as well Emad. Hope to see more of you."

Emad smiled and nodded, but he didn't want to see more of Bob. The bus ride brought back too many painful memories. Next time he'd drive.

Emad's step quickened as Jahana's building came into view. He hadn't seen his daughter in over two weeks. This time of year was busy for her, but for some reason it seemed busier than usual. Every time he called the house, she'd put Cyra or Sahba on to talk, saying she was in the middle of something. He loved talking to his grand-daughters, but missed his daughter. Perhaps this lunch meant things were returning to normal and she'd have more time for him again.

With a smile pasted on his face he opened the door to the faculty offices. Melody, the program assistant, looked up, recognition unfolding in her eyes.

"So good to see you Mr. Agushi. Jahana's in her office. Go on down."

"Please Melody, call me Emad. It's good to see you too."

"It just doesn't seem right. You are Mr. Agushi to me."

Emad grinned and turned down the hall. He paused outside Jahana's partially open office door. The glow of the computer screen illuminated her face. Pride might be one of the greatest sins in Islam, but he couldn't help but be proud of her. A professor, a mother and a wife, but most of all a kind and generous person. He didn't agree with the hijab, but it wasn't his place to interfere in her marriage. She had Noosha's strong will and a piece of cloth hadn't taken that away. She glanced up and a smile spread across her face.

"Baba! How long have you been standing there?" She grinned and wagged a playful finger.

Time stood still as she navigated the desk and side table to embrace him.

"Jahni," he sighed, letting go of the weariness that burdened him. She was his light.

Jahana babbled on about the girls as they strolled arm-in-arm to the cafeteria. Everyone seemed to treat themselves to the mezze platter, but the lines moved quickly and they soon found a table at the back of the room. Other than jostling the crowd, lunch was perfect. Emad dove into his plate, wondering when he last ate a meal that wasn't a peanut butter and jelly sandwich.

"Do you know, Baba?"

Startled, Emad looked up. "Sorry Jahni, I was just enjoying the soothing rhythm of your voice."

"Oh Baba, you were shutting me out and daydreaming!" Jahana pushed him away with a playful shove.

He reached across the table and rested his hand on hers, meeting her gaze.

"No Jahni, I would never shut you out. Now what were you asking?"

Just as he stuffed the last spoonful of tabbouleh into his mouth the conversation turned.

"Tell me about your parents, grandparents and siblings."

Emad's fork paused midway to the table before he set it back on his plate, picked up his napkin and wiped his mouth. His heart beat loudly in his chest. Before speaking, he cleared his throat.

"I taught you to recite the family history word for word. Why are you asking me this?"

Jahana looked down, suddenly interested in her lunch.

"You taught me their names and birth dates. But what were they like? Did they go to the mosque? Do you have any pictures of them? What were their eccentricities?" Then she raised her eyes to meet his. "Who am I most like?"

Emad's heart beat faster. He tried to reason with himself. Jahana always had an interest in family history, that's all this was. But deep down he suspected it had something to do with that DNA test Barid bought. He thought he'd convinced her science wouldn't tell her who she was, but perhaps not.

He coughed and responded in as controlled a voice as he could muster. "What's with all the questions, Jahni?"

"Just curious. The girls are getting bigger and I want to tell them about your family. That's all."

But Emad noticed Jahana dropped her gaze again and was no longer eating. Just pushing food around on her plate with pita bread.

"But you know our family history."

Jahana's eyes jumped fiercely to his. "The facts, Baba, not the details."

Emad sat back, not prepared for Jahana's quick and vehement response.

She tossed the pita bread on top of her food and pushed the plate away. Emad lost his appetite too, slowly folding the napkin and covering his plate. He should ask about the DNA test, but he didn't want to hear the answer.

Jahana glanced at her phone and rose.

"I better get back to work, Baba."

Emad followed carrying the disposable plates, squeezing them into the small slot in the trash on the way out, his stomach growling in protest. The halls seemed silent as they walked back to the office.

Emad knew he disappointed his daughter, but at least he hadn't brought up his disdain for DNA testing and avoided an all-out confrontation.

Jahana turned to him and threw her arms around his middle, before leaving him standing in the hallway. Students rushed past Emad on their way to class. He stared at the faculty office door. *She'd get over it.* He wanted so badly to be part of her life. Why did she think a DNA test could tell her who she was?

The weariness returned as he exited the building and made his way back to the bus stop. He breathed a sigh of relief when a different driver sat behind the wheel of the number four

****

She kept her head down, tears stinging as she rushed back to the office. Melody looked up as she entered from the hall. The front door shut just before she pulled her own office door closed. She collapsed into her office chair, no longer able to stop the tears.

Baba's reaction to her questions telegraphed he hid something. *The Jewish secret?* She felt her face flush as she thought about taking the DNA test. He wouldn't be able to understand her reasons for doing it, and may never forgive her. Getting him to take the test, would be out of the question.

A deep breath caused a shudder to escape. Grabbing a tissue, she wiped her eyes, forcing herself back to work. But before she opened her files there was a soft knock on the door.

"Come in."

Why didn't people just leave her alone? But Melody opened the door, a smile mixed with anxiety pasted on her face. She reached across the desk and handed Jahana an assignment dropped off by a student.

"Is everything okay? Parents aren't always easy to deal with, are they?"

Jahana's face softened. Melody was the one person at the office she could talk to.

"Baba's so stubborn."

Melody handed her a tissue from the box on the side table. "I understand. Dad and I argued over everything. But what I'd give to have him here to argue with today." Her eyes filled with sadness, and she sighed.

Jahana rose and steered her way around the desk, placing a hand on her shoulder.

"I feel the same way about my maman. I rarely argued with her, but what I'd give to have her back." A smile played at the corners of her mouth. "And she'd tell me how to handle Baba."

Melody patted Jahana's hand and turned to leave.

"Thanks for checking on me."

Melody paused and turned. "Just delivering that assignment. Do you want the door closed?"

Jahana hesitated. Fridays were the day she caught up with colleagues. But today she didn't want to chat with anyone.

"Please, I need some alone time."

The door slid shut, rattling thin walls. There was no way to close it quietly.

With another sigh she sat down to prepare lectures for the Feminism in the 21st Century course. It was a surprise to her students that a woman wearing a hijab taught this course. It took a good part of the semester to garner their confidence and help them understand that having the choice as to whether to wear the hijab or not was a feminist issue. Banning the wearing of the hijab was as oppressive as being forced to wear it. She felt a bit hypocritical because she wore hers as a compromise in her marriage.

The unmistakable ring tone of her cellphone startled her. She snatched it up and answered quickly.

"Is everything all right Baba?" Jahana's anger dissolved into concern.

There was a pause and definite exasperation in his voice when he replied.

"Of course."

Jahana realized after her mother passed, the parent-child relationship with her baba had reversed. She obsessed about his well-being. And he didn't like it. There was no doubt he was capable of looking after himself, but he aged so much in the last few months. He would never admit to Jahana his wife's death took its toll on him.

Jahana tried not to dote on him and she had done a good job of that over the past few weeks, but still she worried.

"Thank you for meeting me for lunch. Can we follow-up on our conversation?"

Jahana straightened. A small part of her hoped he wanted to answer her questions and maybe even divulge the family secret. But his frustration and anger were tangible before he spoke.

"Are you pursuing that DNA testing nonsense?"

Jahana sighed and leaned against the back of her chair. But before she had time to respond Emad continued.

"Never mind, don't tell me, I don't want to know. You're a grown woman with a husband and children, but you're not too old to listen to your baba. Do not take that DNA test."

"Baba..."

"Let me finish. Taking that test belittles me. I've always raised you knowing your ancestors. As for your maman's side, if she didn't tell you about ancestors it's because there's nothing to know. I married her not knowing much about her past. And if I can do that, then you can let it be. Do not get tested, understand?"

Jahana closed her eyes, glad her office door was closed. She paused and licked her lips; trying to control her response and remember the conflict resolution training she took the previous month.

"Baba, I can't promise you that. And I can't believe you're asking me to go against Barid's wishes. You're putting me in a very awkward situation with ridiculous demands."

Baba interrupted. "This is not ridiculous. Please do as I say. Barid will get over it. Nothing good can come of this, trust me. I have a bad feeling."

Jahana was sure it was more than a bad feeling, he knew something. There was so much she wanted to say, but she stopped herself.

"Oh Baba, I'll think about it, but that's all I can promise."

Without saying goodbye, he hung up. Her answer wasn't truthful, but it was the best she could do without revealing she'd already taken the test, twice. She wished she hadn't.

Why did her baba think he could control her? It wasn't like him. She worried about the secret he was trying so hard to keep buried. Whose Jewish blood was in her veins? Did he know something about her maman and was preserving her secret? Or was it his own past he didn't want uncovered?

By now he should know demands only pushed her in the opposite direction. She would have to find answers elsewhere and as much as she hated to admit it, Mishal was her only hope.

****

"So, what do you think it means?"

The girls laid on either side of her, propped up on pillows as Jahana read a passage from her mother's book. The girls remained silent.

"Okay, what's the quest? What is it they're searching for?" Jahana turned her head from Sahba to Cyra and back again.

"A special bird?" Sahba squinted up at Jahana. Her hands fidgeted with the blanket.

"Yes, a very special bird. What makes it special?" Jahana wanted to tell them what she had come to learn by reading the book, but she knew it had to come from them.

"Would it be like their God bird?" Cyra raised her hands in the air and separated them like she was revealing something momentous.

"Exactly. That's what I think the quest is all about too. Finding God. You know how we refer to God in many ways?"

The girls nodded.

"So, tell me what other names do we call God?" Jahana turned her head to look at each of the girls.

Sahba was the first to respond. "The King. Or the Holy."

Cyra chimed in. "Allah, or the Most Merciful."

"Good examples. So, in the book, the birds just have their own name for God, the Simurgh."

"Do they find God?" Sahba propped herself up on an elbow and faced Jahana.

"Now that's what we have to read the book to find out. Because it's about more than what they find. It's also about what they learn along the way. If we skipped to the end, we'd miss the journey." As the words fell from Jahana's mouth, the irony wasn't lost. She just wanted to find out where her Jewish genes came from. She didn't want to take the journey, learning the painful lessons along the way.

"What do you think it will take for them to find the Simurgh?"

"Birdseed?"

Jahana faced Sahba and held back her smile. "Now let's be serious. To go on such a long journey what will they need in here?" Jahana placed her palm on Sahba's chest.

"Love?" Cyra sat up. "And all those other things you talked about the other day."

"Oh, you were listening. Well done Cyra." Jahana tucked a stray wisp of hair behind Cyra's ear. "Do you remember any of the other things?"

"Smartness. They'd need to be smart, right Maman?" Sahba sat up too, bouncing up and down.

"Yes! Knowledge, you're absolutely right." Jahana beamed. She'd worried they were too young to understand.

"I don't think this is one of the things you said, but they would have to be patient." A furrow formed between Cyra's eyebrows.

"You're right, it would take a lot of patience. I'm impressed girls. So, you see the birds are going to head out on a quest, a journey, to find the Simurgh. It will be a long and difficult quest, and they'll have to open their minds to possibility. Don't you want to find out what they learn along the journey? Learn about the Valleys they have to go through to get to the end?"

It was Sahba's turn to roll her eyes. She threw herself back onto her pillow. "But it's so boring. Can't you just tell us the ending?"

Jahana reached across Cyra and set the book down on the nightstand. She rolled to face Sahba, raising her hand above her, wiggling her fingers. "Boring? Did you say boring?" She brought her hand down to Sahba's tummy. She could feel her muscles tighten under her flannel nighty.

Sahba grabbed her arm, trying to push the wiggling fingers away as she squealed. "Stop, stop! Not bored, not bored!"

Jahana paused, then both girls were on top of her. Tickling her in return. Squeals and laughter filled the room until a voice cut through.

"What's going on in here?" Barid stood in the doorway, hands on his hips, a smile playing at the corners of his mouth.

"Baba!" The girls rolled off the bed and ran to him. He kneeled and they leaped on him.

Jahana sat up and swung her legs over the side of the bed, tucking the book in her nightstand drawer. She smoothed the covers, lost in thought about the journey that lay ahead of her.

****

Mishal waited in the cafeteria for Jahana. It had been a week since they talked on the phone and assumed that if she hadn't heard anything different, their coffee date was still on. She was early and secured a table at the back, near the window, sending a message to let Jahana know where she was. It wasn't long till she saw her emerge from the cashier's line with a coffee in hand.

"Oh Mishal, so great to see you. It's been too long cousin." Jahana set her coffee on the table as Mishal rose.

They embraced and Mishal noticed Jahana held her a little tighter and longer than usual. It was obvious Jahana missed her too.

"My boss just scheduled a meeting at ten, so I have to leave in fifteen minutes instead of twenty. So sorry, 1 wish I had more time to talk. Maybe we can squeeze in another coffee early next week too?"

"Well, let's get to it then. How have you been? What's kept you so busy?" Mishal took a sip of her coffee and looked at Jahana, trying to read her expression.

Jahana shifted in her seat and her gaze focused just past Mishal. "I'm sorry for being so busy. I've researched my ancestry, and it's just consumed me."

That was it? Relief washed over Mishal, but something didn't sit right. How had researching ancestry caused her to cancel so many coffee dates?

"What do you know about our babas' parents in Iran and their brothers in the United States?" Before Mishal could respond, Jahana continued. "And have you ever seen pictures of them? Other than birth facts and that kind of thing, what else do you know about them?"

Mishal's brows knit and she raised her hand in front of Jahana to quieten her.

"Why are you asking these questions? We both know the same things. Our babas raised us on stories about relatives."

"But do you know for sure that our grandparents can trace their lineage back to Muhammad? That we are truly Sayeed?"

Mishal's jaw dropped. "Are you kidding? Our ancestors trace back hundreds of years in Iran. What's gotten into you? What've you found out in your ancestry search?"

A quiver ran up Mishal's spine. The person sitting in front of her wasn't acting like the cousin she knew.

Jahana turned her gaze to the window. Mishal softened and reached across the table placing her hand on Jahana's.

"What's with all the questions? You've never questioned our lineage before. Why do you question it now?"

Jahana met Mishal's gaze. But she remained silent.

"You can talk to me."

Jahana stiffened. Her mouth opened and closed. Finally, she managed to speak. "Never mind. Forget I asked, it doesn't matter." Jahana slid her hand out from under Mishal's and rested it in her lap.

"What I should ask about is how Adar is doing? Did you get things sorted out at school?"

Mishal ignored her queries.

"Of course, it matters. It clearly matters to you. What's going on Jahana?"

Jahana looked at her phone and jumped to her feet.

"Sorry Mishal. I have to get to that meeting. I shouldn't have brought this up. Please forgive me." Before Mishal responded, Jahana left, the cafeteria door swinging shut behind her.

Mishal's stomach turned. How could Jahana treat her this way? *After a month of no communication this was it? An ancestry inquisition for no apparent reason? And a couple after-*

thought questions about Adar to deflect her away from finding out the real reason for the questions?

Mishal rose from the table, threw her coffee cup in the trash and pushed the door open into the hall with more force than she intended. By the time she reached her car she was trembling. Sitting behind the wheel she took a deep breath and analyzed the conversation.

Jahana cared for her and her family. She always treated the boys like they were her own. There was more going on than she revealed. Mishal's anger turned to worry. Was she using the ancestor thing to cover up what was really wrong? Perhaps she was having trouble in her marriage. That wouldn't surprise her. Or maybe one of the girls was sick, and that was what was instigating the ancestry questions?

As much as her anger tempted her to distance herself from Jahana, Mishal knew she needed to reach out. Jahana needed a friend. She pulled out her phone and texted.

I'm sorry I was no help with the ancestry questions. Maybe we can get together early next week? I'm worried. I'm here for you regardless of what's troubling you.

The shaking subsided. She turned the key in the ignition and backed out of the parking stall. She'd get to the bottom of Jahana's troubles, but it had been a tough week.

Life just never seemed easy.

CHAPTER FIVE

J ahana arrived at the cafeteria early Tuesday morning and glanced at her watch. Did she have time to go back to the office and exchange books for her next class? At least she brought the DNA kit and didn't have to go to the office first. She opted to grab lunch and settle in.

She wished she'd asked about Adar sooner on Friday. *It should have been my first question? How could I be so self-centred?* She'd try to make it up to her.

Mishal scanned the cafeteria and waved when she spotted Jahana.

She doesn't seem angry. Jahana rose and wrapped her arms around her cousin. "Thank you for coming. I'm so, so sorry about my thoughtlessness. Please let me make it up to you."

When they released, she noticed a tear in Mishal's eye.

"Oh cousin. I'm so sorry. Please tell me about Adar. How's he doing? What's the school done about the bullying?"

The women sat down across the table from one another.

"Adar's furious with me. He's upset we involved the principal. He claimed the note was a joke." Mishal took a sip of coffee and leaned back. "But at least the school's taking it seriously. The other parents met with us, they seemed mortified. Now Adar claims he's lost a good friend."

"Adar will come around. You did the right thing, and it's great the school is serious about it. Are you okay though?"

Mishal wiped tears from the corners of her eyes. "Oh yes, the tears aren't about Adar, they're about you. I'm worried and so sorry we argued."

"And I'm sorry too. Barid's anniversary gift has pre-occupied me."

Mishal's eyes narrowed and her soup spoon stopped midway to her mouth.

Jahana continued. "It wasn't the most romantic gift. He gave me a DNA testing kit."

Mishal rolled her eyes, but leaned in to listen.

56

"The results came back a few months ago, but I was sure they were a mistake, so I bought another kit. I received those findings last month, and they confirmed the first ones. It's strange none of the cousin matches have familiar names and there's a peculiarity I want to follow up."

Jahana paused, taking stock of Mishal's reaction. But she showed no emotion.

"Baba knows I received the kit but doesn't know I've taken it. In fact, he's forbidden me to take the test saying it's an affront to him. But I wanted to find some of Maman's relatives, so I took the test despite his words. Now instead of finding relatives, I'm trying to piece together a puzzle."

"That's crazy. What are the weird results?" Mishal dipped the spoon back in her soup and raised it to her lips.

"That's the thing. I can't tell you." Mishal choked on her soup and took a sip of water before leaning back in her chair. Jahana held her hand up between them. "There's no reason for you to know. But I need to ask you a favour."

Mishal tilted her head and eyed Jahana with suspicion.

"I've purchased another kit and want you to take the test. It's the only way I'll know which side of the family the weird results come from. Baba will never take the test, but if you do, I'll be able to figure things out. You only have to spit in a tube."

Jahana reached into her bag, pulled out the kit and placed it in the centre of the table. Mishal leaned further back in her chair and stared at it before raising her gaze to Jahana. "You know I'd do anything for you, but I need to know what those results showed before I take the test.

You're frightening me by keeping them secret. If you're so unhappy about the findings, I don't want to learn what my DNA has to say about me."

Jahana sighed. She wrestled with the idea of telling her everything. But stopped short. If she told Mishal, it would change her world too. There was no sense upsetting her when chances are the Jewish genes ran on her mother's side of the family.

"No problem." Jahana took the box off the table and held it in her lap. "Don't do anything you don't want to. Maybe I need to forget this whole thing. The only reason I wanted to get to the bottom of it was for Cyra and Sahba's sakes. I thought it important they know about their ancestors."

"Just tell me! What could be so bad you can't tell your best friend?"

"Sorry. I understand why you don't want to take the test without knowing my results. But I can't talk about them right now. Maybe someday I will."

"No, Jahana I'm sorry. Sorry you can't trust me." Mishal's face flushed, and she reached for her purse.

Jahana's heart beat in her ears. "It's not a matter of trust, Mishal, I trust you. There's no reason for you to know this unless it ends up affecting you. And it won't. The results probably came from Maman but I don't know any of her relatives to check her side. I thought I'd rule out Baba's family before I try to figure out how to delve into the other side. Maybe someday if I solve the puzzle, I'll let you in on it. Right now, though, there's no sense you worrying about something you don't need to."

"I'm sorry Jahana, but I only think it's fair you tell me your results before I make my decision. If the results are that devastating, I'm not sure I want to take the test." With that Mishal rose and walked out of the cafeteria.

Jahana sat in silence still holding the box under the table. It was small, weighed next to nothing, yet it felt heavy in her hands. She tucked it in her bag and left the cafeteria, stopping at her office. The only way forward would be to tell Mishal the entire story. But learning Jahana was Jewish was not something Mishal could ever unlearn. *How can I ask her to keep a secret that big?*

As she walked to class, Jahana reasoned with herself. Perhaps the best thing was to let it all go. Barid hadn't re-opened discussions about the results, and he likely never would. Maybe her girls didn't need to know about their Jewish ancestry. No one needed to know.

Jahana turned the corner. Students milled about the classroom door. She pulled out the key, unlocked the door, and the students filed in. Perhaps life could return to normal. She enjoyed her life. Over time the results would become less and less important. *Stay focused, those results don't matter one bit.*

The uneasy feeling in the pit of her stomach, however, reminded her otherwise.

****

Emad lay in bed, oblivious to the day. With the blinds down and the curtains drawn, it might have been the middle of the night. He found the darkness soothing. It was much easier to lie in the dark than to face another day without Noosha. He thought back to how they met in university. The first thing he noticed about her was the light that shone from within, an infectious kindness and humility. Everyone wanted to be with her and she made everyone feel special. He wondered why she chose him, but when asked, she claimed he chose her. Truth was she had the pick of the litter, and he always felt she picked the runt.

He spent his life proving she made the right decision. And their love grew. Tehran was a progressive place when they fell in love. But there were problems too, and they made plans to emigrate. His brother was already in Canada which would make for an easier transition. Then Noosha became pregnant. They worried this would delay their plans, but things seemed to fall into place. Jahana gave them a reason to continue with their plans and helped them heal after the loss of their son.

How many times did they say, 'We need to get through this phase and things will be better?' But in hindsight he would give anything to return to those days. Any of them. None were as hard as living without Noosha.

He rolled over and pulled the pillow over his head. Maybe he'd spend the rest of the day in bed, in the dark, hiding from life. The muffled ringing of the phone penetrated the pillow. He wrestled with the idea of letting it ring through. They could leave a message. But curiosity overtook him and he reached for it. The LED display informed him it was Jahana. He cleared his throat and picked it up.

"Hello Jahni, how are you on this fine day." His voice sang out too exuberantly. He hoped she didn't notice, and he hoped it was a fine day, but he didn't know if the sun shone or not.

After their visit at the cafeteria, Emad fell into a bigger slump. Jahana and her girls were his life. He didn't want that to change, and he feared it might if she went through with that ridiculous DNA test. *What would I do if I lost her too?* By the sound of her voice on the other end of the phone, there was no trace of animosity or anger. Had she let it go?

"Would you like to come over on Thursday evening for a barbecue and see the girls?" Jahana's voice was pure bliss.

Emad paused. He loved to spend time with Jahana and the girls, but he felt conflicted. Before Noosha died, he always looked forward to visiting Jahana. The house brought back so many memories of the years they spent together. Since Noosha's passing, however, he found it more difficult. It was bittersweet. He wanted to remember, and yet somehow, he also wanted to forget. He reasoned with himself that the last time he was there it didn't hurt as much. But he didn't want to let go. He wanted it to keep hurting. He needed life to go on and as long as the hurt was raw, moving forward was slow.

"That would be lovely." Emad responded despite his trepidation. "What can I bring?"

"Not a thing! Barid will barbecue lamb chops and I'll make a salad. So glad you can make it Baba."

He hung up the phone and contemplated pulling the pillow back over his head, but he needed to fight the darkness that kept creeping into the room, into his mind. The darkness that produced thoughts that weren't right. Thoughts about what it might be like on the other side with Noosha. How much easier it might be. How much happier he'd be. What a relief to let the darkness take him away. The thoughts were soothing and hypnotic. Succumbing to them would be easy. And yet he fought. For what? What was he fighting for? The darkness would be an easy escape. The path leading to who knows where.

Take the dark path. You won't regret it.

And yet regret wasn't what it was about. A tiny speck of life still gnawed at him like a piece of gravel in a sandal that just won't fall away. Annoying him until he stopped, took a breath and readjusted. Set himself on another trajectory. Pushed through the darkness and searched for the light. Jahana was his light, and he struggled to fight the dark.

His legs swung over the side of the bed and he sat up before he changed his mind. *Today I'll chase the light.*

He picked up the phone and called his doctor. This was depression. Noosha would scold him for not trying to do something. There were things he could do to help himself, but he was almost at the point of not caring enough to pursue them. Thoughts of Noosha pushed him to reach out for help. What would she think of him if he gave up? He'd never forget Noosha's pleading eyes when she asked him to carry on. She knew he would struggle. Jahana was his reason to live. He would cling to her and hope she continued to love him back. No matter what.

****

Cyra and Sahba looked at her like she'd lost her mind.

"Okay, think of it this way. When we make a campfire, it starts with a lot of smoke, right?"

The girls nodded.

"But when the fire burns really hot, the smoke disappears."

Again, the girls nodded.

"But what does that have to do with love?" Cyra flung her arms in the air, exasperated.

"If we think of reason as smoke and love as fire, when love burns brightly, reason is nowhere to be seen." Jahana paused, the girls looked at her with blank expressions.

"Okay, think about it. When a baby is born, they are attached to their mother by pure love. They have no ability to reason, they just love. But as they grow, they become distracted by the things their mother gives them or doesn't give them. They start reasoning about their love. For example, they might think, if Maman lets me go to the mall with my friends I'll really love her. But if she won't let me go, I'll be angry with her. Love becomes a negotiation with oneself. Reason clouds the purity of love."

Cyra nodded. "Oh, I get it. But does that mean I'm a bad person because I let what people do or don't do affect how I feel about them?"

"Not at all. It just means you're human. But loving without judging is something we can all work on. And this ancient poem is trying to teach us that. When we love without reason, we are successfully moving through the Valley of Love on our quest to find our spiritual guide."

Sahba flung herself at Jahana wrapping her arms around her neck. "I love you Maman."

Jahana squeezed her back. "And I love you Sahba." She winked at Cyra and motioned for her to join in the hug. "I love you too Cyra."

Cyra piled on. Sahba let go and pushed away.

"Why can't you let me hug you Sahba?" Cyra rolled onto her back, head resting on Barid's pillow.

"I don't like hugs. They make my skin crawl."

Cyra rolled her eyes and Sahba continued. "But it doesn't mean I don't love you."

Jahana clamped a hand to her chest. These were the moments she lived for. She never had a sister to love or fight with and sometimes she thought it lucky she didn't have to share her love with her parents. Although Sahba didn't understand the poem to the same extent Cyra did, it was clear she was getting something from it.

"That's it Sahba, that's loving without attaching a reason."

Cyra rolled her eyes and sat up. "Can I go to bed and read now?"

Sahba didn't wait for Jahana's answer. She scrambled off the bed and down the hall.

"Yes, you can."

Cyra rose slowly. "Why isn't Baba home before we go to bed anymore."

"Oh honey, he's really busy at work, that's all. He'd rather be here with us."

Cyra nodded and shuffled to the door, turning back to Jahana. "Thanks for teaching us about the poem. I'm starting to like it."

"I'm so glad you do. I know it's difficult and I don't pretend to completely understand it, but it reminds me to try to be a better person. Now off to bed. I'll come say goodnight in a few minutes."

Cyra disappeared down the hall. Jahana sighed. She couldn't help thinking about her own maman. How many times had she let reason cloud her love? And now she was gone. She needed to remind herself that on this journey to find the truth about who she was, she needed to continue to love without reason. Secrets were kept from her, but she loved her baba no matter what she discovered. Love without reason.

It was a good mantra to live by.

CHAPTER SIX

Y ear-end school activities kept Mishal busy in June. She enthusiastically accepted Jahana's invitation to camp with the girls and Uncle Emad the first week of July. The camping trip turned out to be the highlight of their summer. As the week progressed the sadness in Uncle Emad's eyes was replaced with a sparkle. The kids loved listening to his stories, and he loved teasing them.

The infamous marshmallow fight of the camping trip happened on the first night of the trip. Mishal smiled thinking about the look in Cyra's eyes when she realized the marshmallow from her stick had somehow flown across the fire and landed square in her babayi's chest. Uncle Emad sprang to action, flicking his stick and flinging his marshmallow back at her. Soon halal marshmallows were flying everywhere. It was a sticky mess to clean up, but the laughs were worth it.

As Mishal drove home at the end of the week, exhausted but re-energized, she couldn't help but wonder how DNA testing might change family relationships. She was grateful for the bonding time. Soon Jahana's secret would become her secret too. She prayed it wasn't as big as her cousin made it out to be. *Was she over-reacting?* Unlikely. Jahana was the steady, level headed one. Whatever she discovered in her DNA was sure to have a profound effect on all their lives.

I hope the problem comes from Aunt Noosha's family. Mishal's face flushed with guilt, but she had her sons to think about. Whatever the secret was, if it affected her, it would affect her boys.

Mishal recalled the disappointment she felt when Jahana first asked her to have her DNA tested but wouldn't tell her why. Until that conversation she didn't think there was anything they couldn't tell each other. But a few days later, she realized she also disappointed herself. Didn't she trust Jahana enough to take the DNA test? Jahana would never ask her to do something that wasn't important. And so, she had relented on one condition; Jahana promised to share her results once Mishal's results came in. Seven weeks from the time she was tested would take her well into July.

She had never wished July away before. It was her favourite month. But those seven weeks were excruciatingly slow. Mishal checked her account every day, but the results were delayed. It was the 28th of July when they showed up in her inbox. Normally she wouldn't have been indoors during the day, but it was humid, too hot to be outside so the boys played video games and Mishal tidied the house. She was scrubbing the kitchen sink when her phone, sitting on the kitchen counter beside her, showed the email alert from the DNA testing company. She peeled off her rubber gloves and dried her hands on the towel hanging from the cabinet just below the sink. She forced herself to wait for her laptop on the makeshift office space in the kitchen nook to come to life, not wanting to sift through results on her phone. Sweat trickled down her neck, she drew in her breath, then clicked on the link.

Her results stared back from the screen. Was she interpreting the results correctly? She reviewed them a few times, still puzzled. Clearly, she would have to figure out a way to meet up with Jahana, just the two of them, no kids or husbands.

Results are in. Can we meet for lunch tomorrow?

Mishal barely had the message typed when her phone rang.

"I can't wait. Read me your results." Jahana's voice shook.

Mishal contemplated doing as Jahana asked, but took a deep breath instead. "When I agreed to be tested you promised we'd share our result in person, compare them side by side." Mishal was as anxious as Jahana to discuss the results, but she wanted to be sure Jahana didn't back out of their deal.

"Oh, come on Mishal, we've waited so long. Just tell me. Anything unusual?"

"Just meet me for lunch tomorrow and we'll compare."

"I can't. It's the weekend. Barid will be home and I don't want him knowing anything about this." Jahana paused. Mishal heard her take a deep breath before she added, "It'll have to be Monday. Let me know where and when and I'll be there."

****

The rain on Monday morning cleared the air of the humidity, but the tension hung thick. Jahana needed to find a release too. She tossed and turned the last two nights thinking about Mishal's test results. Today, over lunch, they'd know each other's results. Jahana prayed she didn't share her Jewish ancestry. *Please let it come from Maman's side.*

It was unlikely her baba carried the Jewish genes. But Mishal's refusal to talk about the results over the phone was so cryptic. Did she know her secret?

Jahana rose, busying herself with household chores, ending with a quick shower. The girls took advantage of a lazy summer day, remaining in bed.

Jahana stood outside Cyra's door and tapped lightly before entering. "Cyra, time to get up. It's almost afternoon. I'm heading to the Canal Ritz to meet Aunt Mishal for lunch. When I get home, we'll go to Mooney's Bay for a few hours if the rain has stopped like they say it will."

Cyra rolled over and shielded her ears with her pillow. Jahana contemplated a fight, but decided instead to leave her and continued to Sahba's room.

Sahba lay in bed reading. Jahana knelt down and kissed her cheek. "Good morning lazy bones."

Sahba brows furrowed but she didn't look up.

"Okay, I'll leave you to it. I'm off to meet Aunt Mishal for lunch. When I get back, we'll go to the beach."

Sahba glanced at her, then continued to read her book. Jahana backed out of the room and sighed. When did her little girls' exuberance turn into pre-teen indifference?

****

Jahana arrived at the restaurant early, taking a table overlooking the canal. It would have been so much better if they could sit on the patio. But the rain foiled those plans. Droplets collected on the window and paused before sliding down. Jahana inhaled and glanced around the room. The lunch crowd filed in. It would fill soon, especially with the patio closure.

Jahana's phone buzzed, and she flipped it over.

Running behind. Babysitter showed up late.

Jahana replied with a thumbs up, but that's not how she felt. She set the phone down, another sigh escaping her lips.

"Anything I can get you?"

Jahana smiled at the waitress. Her stomach groaned.

"Some lemonade?" Usually she'd wait for Mishal, but she didn't know how late she'd be. Her fingers tore at the napkin. She smoothed it out, placed it on her lap and pulled out her tablet. She noticed the Wi-Fi password on her way in. *Beginnings*. Perhaps a little too appropriate. Her bowels rumbled, and she craned her neck to see the washroom sign. Back out the way she came in. She made it before her bowels spasmed.

Jahana returned to the table scanning the restaurant for Mishal. Just as she sat down, she spotted her at the door.

They hugged before Jahana pulled back and looked into her eyes. She wasn't giving anything away.

"So nice to see you my cousin." Mishal removed her raincoat and they settled into their chairs across from each other.

"So, ma'am, what can I get you to drink?" The waitress set Jahana's lemonade in front of her and turned to Mishal.

"Water, thanks." The waitress smiled and removed the unused wine glasses from the table.

"I'll be back for your order."

Jahana wanted to tell her they'd be awhile, but she'd keep circling until they ordered, so she opened her menu.

"Let's figure out what we're eating before we get into the results." It was all she could do not to reach for her cousin's iPad. But at the same time, she wasn't in a hurry to reveal her own results. And she prayed one more time that Mishal's results held no surprises. Mishal didn't need to be thrown into her turmoil.

"Oh cousin, are we ready for this?" Mishal reached out and held Jahana's hand. She felt the blood drain from her face. *Mishal must be Jewish too.* She took a long slow drink of lemonade. It bubbled up from an already acidic stomach. She swallowed and closed her eyes. B*reathe.*

"Are we ready ladies?" Jahana's eyes snapped open. It was the waitress wanting to take their orders.

Mishal looked at her with concern, then turned to the waitress and smiled. "The soup and sandwich special please."

"Will that be white, whole wheat, multigrain or rye bread?" *Could she go away?* She didn't hear Mishal's answer and realized the waitress was looking at her.

"The same." Jahana closed her menu and handed it to the waitress. *Now just go away and take your time.*

Mishal moved her chair next to Jahana and tapped her iPad, squeezing her arm. "I'll show you my results but I want to make sure you still promise to show me yours?"

Jahana smiled weakly. "I promised when you took the test. I wouldn't go back on that."

The Wi-Fi was slow, but eventually the genetic testing website opened and Mishal clicked on her DNA tab.

Jahana's expression did not waver as she scanned the screen. She remained neutral, clasping Mishal's hand more tightly.

"Thank God," she whispered.

Mishal's results held no trace of Jewish ancestry.

"Okay Jahana. Enough of this. What is it your results show that mine do not? I've looked over my results repeatedly searching for clues to the secret you're keeping. What could it be?"

Jahana turned over her tablet and opened the site. Mishal scanned the results. She glanced at Jahana, her mouth opened, then closed and she looked back down at the tablet. When she raised her head, her brows furrowed and she shrugged her shoulders. Again, her lips opened and closed without uttering a word.

Jahana pointed to the results that indicated she was Jewish. "As you can see I'm Jewish and since you aren't, it means my Jewish genes came from Maman. I was pretty sure this would be how it would turn out, but I had to be sure it wasn't Baba's side."

Mishal touched Jahana's hand, her eyes searching Jahana's face. "But why wouldn't you tell me you have Jewish ancestry. It's not like that would bother me. You know that don't you?"

Jahana clasped her hand. "Oh, I know it wouldn't be a problem for you, but I didn't want you knowing my truth and having to keep my secret. And I'm sorry you're now in that position." Jahana let out a long slow breath.

"Why don't you just talk to your baba?" Mishal stroked Jahana's arm, tears pooling.

"He's been so adamant about forbidding me to get tested, there's got to be more to this. I don't understand why either of my parents would have kept this secret from me. And now I have Barid to deal with."

Mishal clamped a hand over her mouth. "Barid. Of course. That's really why you're worried. I assume you haven't told him?"

"Here you go ladies. Fresh pepper for either of you?" The waitress set down the soup and sandwiches and Mishal moved her chair around to her place setting, declining the pepper. Jahana shook her head, not bothering to speak.

Once the waitress moved away, Jahana leaned towards Mishal, careful not to drag her hijab through her soup. "I haven't told Barid, but he's likely to bring up the testing at some point. He gave me the test after all. I didn't want you knowing because it's a secret that will be hard to keep to yourself. And I know you won't tell anybody; I just didn't want you to have this secret no one else can know."

"I won't breathe a word, promise. Are you going to talk to your baba about it?"

"I don't think I can. Even though it's Maman's side carrying the Jewish genes, he must know. He's been so adamant about me not getting tested. He's used the word 'forbid', even though he knows the kit was a gift from Barid." Jahana's stomach rumbled, and she opened the package of crackers hoping they'd sop up the acid.

Jahana held back tears. This would not be a pity party. She shrugged. "My gut says it won't be good. He's irrational. Being raised in Palestine gives him a different perspective. He doesn't differentiate between Israelis and Jews, he thinks they're all the same and blames them for the strife his family continues to endure. But does that mean he'll hate me? I can't say. I fear more for Cyra and Sahba. How will his feelings change towards his own children?"

The cracker was helping to settle her stomach. Or was it having someone to confide in? There was no judgement from Mishal. She knew there wouldn't be. And she was so glad Mishal's results held no surprises. Not that Hamid would react anything like Barid.

"Could your baba's reaction be a legitimate Muslim father's ego, not wanting you to question the ancestry he's given you?" Mishal took a bite of her chicken salad sandwich.

Jahana shook her head. "No, I'm sure it's more than that. He's told me not to look for my maman's relatives.

Something's not right." Jahana dipped a cracker in the tomato soup before raising it to her mouth. The acid of the tomato caused her stomach to spasm. She pushed the bowl away and looked at the sandwich before raising her eyes to Mishal.

"You understand why I have to pursue this don't you? Cyra and Sahba have a right to know their ancestry before they get into relationships. How will I ever tell Barid? He'll be so angry that no one told him before our wedding."

Mishal's eyes widened, before she looked down.

Jahana divulged Barid's potential anger before thinking. She never told Mishal about the side of Barid only she saw. But she knew Mishal suspected how he acted behind closed doors. And it felt good to talk to someone about it.

Jahana continued. It was like the flood gates opened and she couldn't stop talking about all the things she kept to herself. "My maman never talked about her family. Guess it makes sense now. But why didn't she? My baba's a liberal Muslim, and his response to my DNA kit makes me think he knew he married a Jew. And she practiced Islam. Conversion of a Jew to Islam wouldn't have been an issue for him." Jahana paused and stared at her friend listening intently, not interrupting.

"I've never doubted my baba's love for my maman. They were soulmates. Religion wouldn't have torn them apart. But why did they keep a Jewish background from me? It doesn't make any sense. If I'd known, Barid and I would never have been married."

Mishal touched her hand. "But if you'd known, you wouldn't have Cyra and Sahba."

Jahana sat back in her chair. "Trust me, I've thought of that. And for that reason alone, I'm glad I didn't know. Still, my life is such a mess now."

Mishal folded her napkin and placed it on her plate, rose and slid her chair to Jahana's side of the table.

"Let's compare our matches. That should tell us which ones are relatives from your Maman's side." Jahana pushed her bowl and plate aside and pulled out her iPad.

"This is weird, it doesn't appear we have any common matches. But I see names of cousins on your matches I recognize. Look there's Abby from San Francisco." Jahana's brows knit and she looked at her cousin, puzzled.

Mishal's face dropped, turning pale. She grabbed Jahana's tablet and scrolled through her results before placing it back in her lap. "It's not just that. There's something else missing. We aren't matches to each other."

Jahana's eyes widened and her bowels constricted. "We aren't cousins. Baba's not my biological father."

CHAPTER SEVEN

J ahana stared at the sky, a mound of sand her pillow as the girls played in the water. She fought the tears stinging her eyes. *Barid will see me not only as a Jew, but also a bastard. Am I making this bigger than it needs to be? Will he really see me that way?*

She kept her promise of a trip to Mooney's Bay, but all she wanted to do was lay in bed and cry. There was no time for self-pity. She closed her eyes; wild crazy thoughts ran through her mind creating chaos as she wrestled with the anger burning deep inside. Her hands trembled. She interlaced her fingers across her abdomen, knuckles turning white. This was too much. Her parents kept secrets from her, important secrets. It wouldn't hurt so much if she hadn't been close to them, but they were close. What reason did they have to lie to her? Something just didn't add up.

"Maman, come in. The water's beautiful!" Jahana raised her head and shaded her eyes. Sahba was waving at her from the water's edge.

She waved back shaking her head. "I didn't bring my burkini." Sahba's smile disappeared, and she sat in the water. Jahana laid her head back down and closed her eyes.

She had always been close to her mother. There were those few weeks in grade eight they didn't see eye to eye, but other than that their relationship was envied by many. Their souls didn't just touch, they intertwined. Jahana wasn't sure what upset her more, knowing the man who raised her wasn't her biological father or the fact her maman never told her the truth.

Perhaps Baba didn't know either? Recent actions seemed to say otherwise; protests over DNA testing made sense if he knew he wasn't her baba. Did Noosha tell him before she died? He seemed so angry at the time of her mother's death. Was that why? Jahana chalked it up to anger over God taking her too soon. It made her resentful, but was it something more for him? But if it stemmed from learning he wasn't her father; he'd feel guilty about that too and it could add to his sadness. *Am I over-thinking this?*

Jahana's parents' relationship was enviable. It would be hard to believe Baba wouldn't know he wasn't her biological father. Unlike her and Barid, her parents never fought, at least not in front of her. Marriage looked easy, although they told her several times it was hard work. They supported each other and were inseparable. Even Jahana's friends commented on how lucky she was to have parents who loved each other so much.

"I'm bored." Cyra plopped down beside Jahana who lifted her head and squinted.

"Bored? But you're at the beach. Go play with your sister." Cyra plodded off, grumbling. Jahana rested her head again. She should get up and play with them, but she couldn't move her body. She settled back into her thoughts.

Did her baba's reaction over her mother's death stem from a fear of losing Jahana too? Her eyes sprang open and her heart quickened. *What if that was it?* Did he hold the key to the answers she needed? She couldn't ask the questions. He was too fragile right now. She needed to continue treating him like the father he'd always been.

This changes nothing. He's still my father, and always will be. My love for him hasn't changed because some scientist decreed, he's not my biological father.

Science. Hadn't her baba said she didn't need science to tell her who she was? He was right, but he was also wrong. The seed took root. How could she stop the search for answers now? Puzzles were never her thing, and this would be a challenge like no other, figuring out who donated their DNA to her. And who was Jewish? Her mother or her biological father?

Shadows cross over her and she opened her eyes against the bright sky.

"Can we go home?"

Jahana looked from Cyra to Sabha. They had enough beach for the day. She sat up and moved to her knees before rising. When had she gotten so old?

****

Back at the house the girls retreated to the living room to watch a movie. Jahana rummaged through the kitchen cupboard pulling out the popcorn pan. She set it on the burner, adding oil and three kernels of popcorn, still lost in thought.

The only clues she had lay in the cousin matches identified through the DNA testing. But she would be playing Russian roulette. Which ones were related to her mother, and which ones to a biological father she didn't know? While she waited for the pan to heat, she peeked into the living room. The girls sat side-by-side on the couch enthralled in one of her favourite old movies.

Cyra's new bob haircut suited her, and she was growing out of her awkward stage into a tall beautiful teen. Sahba still oblivious to fashion trends and hairstyles, had an undeniable beauty. Dark curly hair framed both of their beautiful flawless complexions, long lashes highlighting huge dark eyes accentuated by a sharp nose. *Which of their features were Jewish? Which features came from her maman?* She settled on the nose. *Was it a Jewish nose?* She always loved her maman's nose and was glad when both girls seemed to inherit it. It was a strong feature. Her stomach lurched. Some of her features must have come from the unknown parent. *Which ones?*

Jahana returned to the kitchen when the three kernels popped, indicating the pan was ready. She scooped out the exploded seeds and poured fresh kernels into the steaming oil. The dip in the centre of the pan was perfect for funneling in the kernels and heating them to just the right temperature. The warped lid didn't fit right, but the chipped knob on top was sturdy enough to hold the lid while shaking the pan. She had popped many kernels in this pan over the years. So had her maman. It was one of her parents' first purchases when they immigrated to Canada.

Juggling serviettes and the popcorn bowl she squeezed between the girls on the couch and watched as the two dogs and cat in *Homeward Bound* found their way back to their family after a long difficult trek. Jahana couldn't help but compare the journey she was about to embark on. Could she even hope for a comparable heartwarming reception at the other end?

CHAPTER EIGHT

The rest of the summer passed quickly. Jahana let her results stay parked until fall and dedicated her days to ensuring the girls enjoyed their summer. One day they would move out and her time with them would be sporadic, an odd weekend here and evening there. She cherished them while they still wanted to spend time with her. They made a few trips: Toronto, Vermont, Montreal, where they'd done a lot of sightseeing, some hiking and even zip-lining just across the river in the Gatineau Hills. And Baba joined them. Time with him proved difficult at first. Jahana expected him to detect she knew the truth about their relationship. But if he ever suspected anything, he never brought it up.

Back at work she prepared for the upcoming term. With no new teaching assignments, her year ahead looked promising. She could build on her work and improve her offerings and be ahead of the curve for the first time in her teaching career.

On this first day back, she had trouble concentrating. She glanced at the clock, lunch time. Laughter filtered down the hall from the coffee room, but she ate lunch at her desk and reviewed her DNA matches on the MyGeneticFamily account. Tomorrow she'd join her colleagues for lunch.

The summer gave her plenty of time to plan how to approach her matches. She studied the names of her cousin matches to figure out which might be Jewish and which might be Muslim. She wanted to concentrate on her mother's ancestors, which she assumed were the source of her Jewish genes. It wasn't a logical assumption, more of a feeling than anything. She didn't want to find the man she couldn't bear to call father or any of his relatives. Baba was the only father she needed.

Not every match on MyGeneticFamily disclosed a name. Some used a combination of letters and numbers and some used cutesy taglines. But some used legitimate names. She'd start with the three second cousin matches.

One of the second cousins used the number-letter combination for a name, but the remaining two had what appeared to be real names. One even had a picture attached to her profile. Jahana wasn't good at seeing similarities in features, and although this woman had dark hair and eyes, her nose was different, almost a pug nose. A private profile didn't allow Jahana to see if she had Ashkenazi Jewish ancestry or not. But this woman appeared to have a common Muslim name, Ahmadi. A married name? Perhaps still Jewish? The other match, Adam Samuelson, while also having a private profile, had a Jewish name.

Jahana hovered the mouse's arrow over the message button and hesitated. This might open more than just an email screen. It might open conversations she didn't want to have. Information she'd wish she never learned. She opened the email and typed before she thought any further.

> *Hello Adam. I see we matched as second cousins on MyGeneticFamily. I'm hoping you can tell me if you know anyone by the name of Noosha Jahakhana or anyone by that last name. She was my mother and I am looking for her relatives. I was born in Tehran in 1979 and I immigrated to Canada a few weeks later. I look forward to hearing how we're connected.*

Too much information? Not enough? Jahana worried her words sounded desperate or not desperate enough to meet relatives. She wasn't looking forward to uncovering their connection. If he wasn't related to her maman, Jahana was reaching out to someone related to her biological father.

She closed her eyes and whispered a prayer aloud. "Please God, connect me to Maman's relatives." Her finger clicked the send button before she spent more time talking herself out of moving forward.

Her maman told her a bit about her family before she died. Jahakhana was her maiden name, not at all Jewish.

84

The Jahakhanas were prominent in Iran before the revolution, and her brother was executed by the Khomeini regime for supporting the deported Shah. After her family fled to all parts of the world out of fear for their safety, her maman lost touch with them. She traded her past for a future with her husband and child and disappeared into the fabric of Canada. The only nod to her family was the name she gave Jahana. Now Jahana wondered if she was digging up something, she would wish she hadn't? If her maman wanted to disappear should Jahana search for her family?

Then again, perhaps her maman wasn't a Jahakhana. Maybe it was all fabricated to hide her Jewish ancestry. It was no secret the Khomeini regime caused the large Jewish population in Iran to flee for their lives. A false identity would make sense. But why pick a name that the regime disliked?

CHAPTER NINE

The sun glowed through the open blinds as Emad faced Noosha's dresses with large garbage bags hanging from clenched fists. She would want him to donate them. She gave to the less fortunate whenever she could and wouldn't be happy her dresses hung in the closet a year and a half after her death.

A deep breath escaped his lips, and he reached for the first hanger. It slid off into his arms and he held it to his cheek, closing his eyes. Imagining. The faint scent of Oscar de la Renta lingered, he didn't count on smells and he fell to his knees cradling the faded cotton floral. Face buried in memories. Willing her back into existence. *Fold and bag.* It took all of his resolve to let go of the dress and repeat with the next dress. Pieces of his heart fell into the bag with each garment. It became a farewell ritual, a long goodbye.

"I will never forget you, Noosha," he whispered as he gently slid clothing from hangers, his fingers absorbing the soft textures.

A sob escaped, but he cleared his throat and squeezed back tears as he tied the last bag. The empty closet rod and line of bags caused his heart to quicken. The Salvation Army would get the donation, but not today. He closed the closet door behind him and turned. The bed beckoned. If he lowered the blinds, he could withdraw into the darkness for a few hours. It would be a relief. He deserved it.

Just for a few minutes...

The antidepressants lifted the darkness, but it crept back in on days like this. Should he do what he wanted to do or the right thing? *I need to be strong.*

With the back of his hand he wiped the tears from his eyes and strode out of the bedroom and down the stairs. On this early September day, he vowed to fight the darkness.

The La-Z-Boy called to him and he obliged. Sitting back, he raised the footrest and phoned Jahana.

"Would it be okay if I came over after school this afternoon for a quick visit? I want to hear all about the girls' first day."

"Of course, Baba. That would be great."

Emad breathed a sigh of relief, proud of himself for shunning the darkness and choosing the light. The pills were largely to thank for being able to do it, but still, he was making headway.

The car pulled in front of his old house just after three. Jahana's car already in the driveway. The girls would be home soon too.

"Hello Baba, the girls will be so happy to see you." Jahana stood on the front step.

Emad enveloped her in his arms before they slipped inside. The smell of fresh bread greeted him. Noosha made bread daily in this kitchen. Ghosts of the past no longer stepped out to greet him, but he felt their presence. Jahana kept the paint colors the same, yellow in the entry, gingerbread red in the living room. Noosha picked those colors from a piece of fabric she fell in love with. Emad's skepticism of the color faded as their warmth made the house cozy. He was glad Jahana thought so too.

"Such a beautiful day Baba." Jahana chattered on with an exuberance that tried too hard. Emad listened, but couldn't help wonder why she didn't seem to be herself. It wasn't that she was unhappy, actually the opposite, she was too happy, too enthusiastic. Somehow, she didn't seem authentic and Emad couldn't put his finger on what was hiding behind her gusto.

Is she this way with everyone, or just me?

The girls burst through the door. "We saw your car." Cyra leaped into Emad's arms, Sahba right behind.

Emad buried his face in their hair. *I'm so glad I fought the darkness today*. But as Cyra and Sahba untangled themselves from his hug, he glimpsed something in Jahana's eye as she turned toward the kitchen. It resembled sadness, and he wondered why. Perhaps she thought of Noosha. But it seemed to be something more

"Stay for dinner, Baba." Jahana turned back to him, the sadness gone.

Did I imagine it? Emad shook his head. "No, no I didn't come to intrude and be a nuisance."

Jahana rolled her eyes. "Oh please, what else do you have planned?" Her words gnawed at his loneliness, but she was just teasing.

"I guess it's time I got a social life outside of you and your family. You don't need to include me in everything."

"Oh Baba, I didn't mean it like that. We love having you here. Will you stay?"

"Not today Jahni. I've got chicken out for dinner. Another time." Emad thought about the peanut butter and honey sandwich he'd have for dinner. Taking care of himself needed to become a bigger priority, including finding some outside interests and meeting new people. Noosha's absence seemed to occupy a larger space when he was around old friends. There were the men at the mosque but their conservative views didn't fit with his more liberal ways.

After a short visit Emad headed home. He flicked the light switch on as soon as he passed through the front door. He wasn't letting darkness back in.

****

"I love summer, but it's nice to be back in a routine and meeting for coffee again on Fridays. I've missed our weekly chats." Mishal grinned across the table at Jahana. Their talks were limited after their reveal, but they vowed to discuss it in the fall. "I still consider you a cousin and always will. The fact we don't share genes has nothing to do with how we're related. You're as much a part of me as anyone else I'm related to."

Jahana opened her mouth to reply but Mishal raised her hand.

"Before you interrupt, I just want to say I understand why you want to pursue the ancestry investigation. But I'm not sure digging up a painful past is necessary."

Jahana breathed deeply and looked up. Mishal continued before Jahana interjected.

"And yes, you want to do this for Cyra and Sahba. But maybe they'll marry husbands that don't care about their background. Do you think risks of marriage problems outweigh the problems this will cause for all of you now?"

Jahana attempted to speak again, but Mishal continued.

"Barid won't be able to let this go, his Palestinian roots run too deep. And your baba? What good will it do him to find out he isn't your baba or, if he knows, realize you're aware too? Without Noosha, he's too fragile. He can't weather another storm." Mishal's eyes implored Jahana to listen.

"Can I speak now?" Jahana's eyebrows raised, her pursed lips melting into a conciliatory smile. Mishal nodded.

"I appreciate your advice. I've thought all of that through, and it's necessary to proceed. In fact, I've already started my investigation."

Mishal shook her head and leaned back in her chair.

"I started by messaging one of the second cousin matches. I picked one with a Jewish name."

Mishal's raised her hand and leaned forward again, determined to understand what Jahana was doing and why. "Hold on, why Jewish?"

"It seems like a long shot, but I'm basing my choice on Maman's nose." Jahana chuckled and paused waiting for Mishal to say something. When she didn't, Jahana continued. "Maman had a sharp nose and many Jewish people do too. So, I'm making a leap here and reaching out to a Jewish cousin, hoping he's related through Maman."

Mishal sat back in her chair and sipped her coffee. "Your maman's nose never struck me as Jewish. But I don't think I've ever really associated a nose type with Jewish. Anyway, did he respond?"

"No, not a word. It's been two weeks. How do I move forward? The only other second cousin match that uses a name on MyGeneticFamily, sounds Muslim." Jahana threw her hands up in frustration and shook her head.

"Again, I'm asking, do you want to proceed with this?" Mishal leaned forward and grasped Jahana's hand. "I mean, aren't you worried about what you'll find? Aunt Noosha spent her life hiding from the Jahakhanas. Do you want to blow that wide open? What nut bars out there still have an axe to grind with any sympathizers to the old regime?"

Jahana moved her hand out from under Mishal's and reached for her coffee. "It's not something I'm worried about. I understand my maman's concern, but the revolution was forty years ago. The Shah is long dead. People have moved on. Jahakhanas aren't on the radar anymore. This secret has gone on long enough. It's time to sort out my ancestors. Cyra and Sahba deserve the truth about who they are." Jahana took a long swallow of coffee, keeping her gaze on Mishal.

"What you'll find and how it'll affect your life, isn't worth the risk. It's noble of you to worry about Cyra and Sahba, but they have good lives. You might change that."

"I'll be careful, I've already thought of all the things you're worried about. I won't reveal what I find until I have some concrete facts. There's a chance I won't even be able to solve this ancestry mystery. But I have to try. If I get the facts, I'll decide what to do with them. Finding out about my biological father doesn't interest me at this point. But someday I might change my mind. Right now, I just want to find my maman's relatives and figure out the Jewish link. What if Maman wasn't a Jahakhana, and that was a story to cover up her Jewish ancestry? Who knows?"

Mishal sensed exasperation in Jahana's voice, and was afraid to push further, but she had to make sure she understood her point of view.

"I have tingles up my spine and dread in the pit of my stomach. I'll support you in whatever you do, but I don't agree with it and I'm worried about what all this digging will uncover. Some things are better left untouched."

One look at her cousin and Mishal realized she'd said too much, but it was too late, it couldn't be unsaid.

Jahana rose from the table, her face flushed and jaw clenched. "I'm sorry you feel that way Mishal, But I've thought this through. Sorry, but I've got to get back to work."

Mishal remained seated. The cool room suddenly very warm. Jahana was so stubborn. While she liked that trait about her, it might be her undoing. Mishal's fear was real. Khomeini executed a Jahakhana. The family was well known as sympathizers to the Shah. Who knew what they'd been up to over the past forty years? Whether or not they were relatives, asking questions about them and digging them up would raise red flags somewhere. Jahana's quest to solve her past, didn't have her thinking about the safety of her or the children. Then again, her mother named her Jahana as a link to her past. Did she hope one day Jahana would find her family? Perhaps Aunt Noosha approved of Jahana's search. Although the mystery father, was another story. If her mother wanted her to know about him, she would have told her. There were too many unknowns. Too much risk. Too much opportunity for things to go off the rails. But with Jahana's resolve, Mishal doubted there was anything anyone could say to dissuade her from this mission.

She vowed to hold her opinions to herself and be the sounding board Jahana needed. She'd keep her judgment to herself.

****

"Understanding, for each traveler, is enduring; but knowledge is temporary…"

Jahana slowed, pausing before she reached the bedroom doorway. The girls were waiting for her to join them, but they started reading without her.

"Okay, stop. What do you think that means?"

"Sahba, if we stop every few words, we're never going to get through it." Jahana' could hear Cyra's sighs from the hallway.

"But Cyra, if knowledge is temporary, why do we go to school?"

"Maybe it's to understand."

Jahana smiled. She could picture the two of them lying next to each other discussing the meaning of the third valley, the Valley of Understanding.

Cyra's answer must have satisfied Sahba, because Cyra's voice continued. "There are different ways of crossing this valley, and all birds do not fly alike."

Jahana stepped into the room. "Look at you two. My maman would be so proud." The girls made room between them and Jahana crawled up the centre of the bed.

"So, what have you learned so far about the Valley of Understanding?"

"That understanding is more important than knowing something." Cyra was quick with her answer.

"And everybody understands differently."

Jahana and Cyra both looked at Sahba. "Wow, you girls are amazing. You're both brilliant! You don't need me reading to you anymore. You've got this stuff figured out."

"No, Maman. I like it when you read better."

Cyra sat up and glared at Sahba.

"I mean, I like it when you read, Cyra, but it's nice when Maman's here too."

Cyra smiled and lay back down.

Jahana read a few more paragraphs, then set the book down. "So, if knowledge isn't enough, but we need to understand too, what do you think the Valley of Understanding is trying to say?"

Both girls remained quiet.

"Okay, let me put it this way. What are they trying to understand?"

"God?" Cyra waved her hand excitedly in the air. "They're trying to not just know there's a God bird, but they're trying to understand what a God bird is."

"And everyone has a different understanding." Sahba sat up her eyes wide with excitement. "Right Maman?"

"I think you both have it figured out. Understanding comes from inside all of us. Things we experience in life changes how we understand. It doesn't mean how I understand God is wrong from the way you understand God, it's just different."

Barid's experiences will shape his understanding. Our perceptions are so far apart. Especially when it comes to Jews. Why didn't I realize these differences could be a problem before we were married?

Cyra nodded slowly. "I think I get it."

"I think you both get it. You amaze me girls. You're way ahead of where I was at your age in your understanding of this poem."

Sahba frowned and pointed at Jahana. "Now Maman, that doesn't mean anything. We all understand differently." Her frown turned into a grin and she backed off the bed and ran down the hall.

"Looks like we're done for the night, Cyra."

Cyra cuddled in and Jahana embraced her and closed her eyes. A hug was just what she needed.

"Are you okay Maman?"

Jahana pulled away, looking into her daughter's eyes. "Of course, why do you ask?"

"You just seem so unhappy and you spend so much time on your computer. You're too busy to spend time with us."

"Oh Cyra, I'm sorry. Things are busy at work and with your baba also being busy, it makes it hard for me to keep up. I promise I'll try harder to spend more time with you."

Cyra slid off the bed and sauntered down the hall.

****

Emad was on his way to Jahana's. When he refused to stay for dinner the previous week, Jahana made a point to invite him specifically for a meal. But she felt a little guilty this evening. His presence was part of her plan. Two Jewish immigrants joined her volunteer group, and she hoped to work in some conversation about them to gauge reactions. It might be a way to find out how much her baba knew about Jews and how intolerant Barid was of them.

Jahana sat at one end of the table, trying to enjoy the girls' enthusiastic chatter. Barid and her baba seemed enthralled in their stories, but Jahana kept looking for an opportunity to talk about Bina and Aviva. It had to be a natural entry, nothing obvious.

"Emad, I have something to ask of you."

Jahana sat up. What could Barid want to ask of her father?

96

Without waiting for her father's acknowledgement, Barid continued. "Would you be able to stay here and watch over Cyra and Sahba next weekend? I'd like to take Jahana away for a little holiday."

Jahana's eyes widened. *What brought this on?* But she remained silent, holding her breath awaiting her baba's response.

"I would love to!"

Cyra and Sahba launched into a frenzy of excitement. Barid eyed Jahana's reaction. She sat still and kept her emotions hidden behind a face feigning a pleasant surprise.

"Where are you taking my lovely daughter?" Emad broke through the excited squeals.

"I thought we might go up to Quebec City for the weekend. Stay at the Chateau Frontenac for a treat. I realized the other day we didn't spend any weekends away together this summer, and it's time we did." His eyes turned to Jahana. She pasted what she hoped was an enthusiastic smile on her face.

"Oh Barid, what a lovely idea. But I have my volunteer work on Saturday mornings and there are two new participants from Iran that rely on these meetings."

She set the bait. Now she needed Barid or her baba to ask about the new participants, but she also worried this roadblock to their weekend away might send Barid into a rage. The rage may not surface just now, but she was certain she'd see it later.

"I already thought about that." Barid smiled. "We'll leave after lunch. I have some work I need to finish Saturday morning, anyway."

The bait didn't work. No one asked about the Iranian participants. Weren't they interested in where they were from in Iran? But Barid hijacked the conversation, turning it back to focus on his agenda. He didn't seem angry, but she could never tell with Barid. It may surface after Baba left, and the girls were in bed. Going away with him was the last thing she wanted to do, but there appeared to be no way out. She would be his captive for the weekend.

"Perfect!" Jahana intoned, hoping she injected the right amount of excitement into that one word. "It will be great for the girls to spend time with you, Baba. Thank you."

Barid's ulterior motive for a weekend getaway worried her. What could he want? A whole weekend together, what would they talk about? What if he brought up the DNA testing? Her intestines clenched. She needed to be ready with answers. Mishal might help her come up with some good responses, just in case.

A weekend away. They hadn't done that in years.

As they crawled into bed, Barid reached across and gripped her shoulder.

This is it, he's angry. Jahana stopped breathing.

But he simply pulled her close and kissed her forehead before rolling over.

What's gotten into him? Was he attempting to re-energize their marriage? But deep down she feared there was more to it than that. The possibilities kept her awake long after his snores filled the room.

Barid never did things without an underlying motive. Especially kind, generous things.

CHAPTER TEN

E mad stroked his coffee cup and fidgeted in his chair.

"Oh Baba, you'll be fine. The girls are older now and take care of themselves. They're so excited to spend the weekend with you. Why don't you come tomorrow night? When Barid and I leave Saturday, you'll be comfortable with everything."

Emad raised the cup and took a sip considering her offer. "That might not be a bad idea. Are you sure it won't be a bother if I sleep over?"

"Baba, you're never a bother." Jahana pushed the plate of cookies across the island.

He wasn't one to turn down a homemade chocolate chip cookie. "And I'm looking forward to spending time with the girls. Noosha did the 'looking after' when we used to babysit. I just played." Emad smiled.

"That's all you'll have to do this weekend too. They're self-sufficient now." Jahana rose and tidied the counter.

Emad joined her, running water in the sink. "Is everything okay Jahni? You seem distracted. I'm worried."

"Yes, everything's fine. Just thinking about all the things to get done before we leave on Saturday."

"But I don't mean right now, you've seemed off for a couple months. Is something bothering you?"

Emad turned and touched her arm causing her to look away and continue to wipe the island.

"No, I'm fine. Some days I take on too much. And there's my volunteer job on Saturdays. The group has grown and the two newest members are Jewish sisters, from Iran." Jahana turned to face him, this time holding his gaze.

His heart pounded in his chest. "So, why's that a problem?" Emad's eyes narrowed. *What was she getting at?*

"Oh, the fact they're Jewish isn't a problem, I just feel like I'm not reaching them. They never contribute to group discussions. Do you have any experience around Jews? Do you think the hijab intimidates them?"

Emad turned back towards the sink and continued scrubbing the cookie sheet. *Did she know something?* He cleared his throat "No, I can't say I've had the pleasure of being around Jews. Perhaps you need to remove the hijab? The regime in Iran has been brutal to Jews, especially those with ties to Israel. A hijab might intimidate them." He turned around to catch her reaction.

Her face flushed, and she waved her hand at him. "Oh, I can't do that. There are men in the class too." Emad looked down, hoping she didn't see his eyes roll. He didn't understand her need to wear the hijab.

"So that's what's been bothering you for months? Reaching out to the Jewish women?" He peered back up, his lopsided grin and cock of the head indicating she hadn't been convincing.

"Yes. And everything else, work, being a Maman and wife. I'm just busy, that's all."

Emad could tell Jahana was about to say something more but stopped. "You're sure there's nothing else?"

Tears formed in the corners of her eyes.

"What is it Jahni? He wiped his hands on the towel and clasped her hands in his.

"Oh, nothing. I just miss Maman."

"Oh Jahni, me too." Something told him that was the tip of the iceberg. But she didn't want to talk about it. Was she having marriage trouble too? Maybe that was what this weekend away was all about?

****

Jahana stared at her computer screen. Adam Samuelson hadn't responded. It was understandable. The hijab in her profile picture made it clear she was Muslim.

Should she contact the other two cousins, Alya Ahmadi and ladywho123? Her fingers drummed the keyboard tray before she copied and pasted the message, she sent to Adam into a new message space for each of the other two cousins. If only they didn't have private profiles, she could see if they had Jewish ancestry. It would make things so much easier. After a few modifications to the messages she pressed send.

The third and fourth cousin matches taunted her. Did she have to reach out to them? She opened up the list when a message alert popped up on her screen indicating she had mail. A response from Alya Ahmadi. Her hand shook. It was that easy? She should have messaged her weeks ago.

> *Hello Jahana. I'm afraid I have little news. I can't figure out how we're related. While I'm not aware of any Jahakhanas in the family, these are the last names that seem to weave themselves through my family tree: Banai, Kamali, Shahzad and Majoub. If you figure out how we're related, please let me know.*

Jahana sat back in her chair and ran her fingers through her hair wondering why it had to be another dead end. *This woman is likely related through my biological father. Not going down that road.*

She shook her head and closed the message. While Alya sounded nice, none of the names were familiar and she didn't want to find out why. She hoped ladywho123 would respond with a more hopeful message.

Jahana took a closer look at the third and fourth cousins. What if she sent messages to the matches that showed significant Jewish ancestry? Why hadn't she thought of this before? She'd been so fixated on second cousins. Out of ninety-eight third to fourth cousins, twenty-five had public profiles. Of these twenty-five, only five had significant Ashkenazi Jewish ancestry results. Jahana sent the five the same message sent to the second cousins and made her profile public. Anyone could see her Jewish ancestry. It was risky, but waiting was tiresome. Time to find her maman's relatives.

Jahana tapped the desk. Now that Alya responded in such a timely manner, she didn't want to leave her computer. While she waited, she messaged Mishal, relaying Alya's response.

Mishal responded immediately.

> *That's too bad Jahana. Sorry it wasn't better news. What are you going to do now?*

Despite Mishal's disapproval of Jahana tracing her ancestry, Jahana appreciated her efforts to be supportive and decided to keep her up to date with her efforts.

> *I've messaged the other second cousin and I've also messaged all third and fourth cousins with Jewish ancestry in their DNA profiles. Just waiting for responses.*

No new messages appeared in the testing site inbox, so Jahana closed down her computer and climbed the stairs to the main floor. Baba's snores echoed down the hall from the spare room. Barid worked late. It was rare for him to get home in time to see the girls before bed, but it bothered her that even on a Friday night he was late. Goosebumps formed on her arms. Something didn't seem right with the way he'd been acting. Quebec City worried her.

Why is he taking me away for the weekend? It wasn't something he'd ever done before. Bags were packed, and ready for a noon departure the next day.

She gave her hands a shake and rolled her shoulders. Maybe it would be nice to get away, a chance to reconnect. She'd try to keep an open mind, but a niggle kept surfacing. As she brushed her hair, she recalled better times. Barid's conservatism inserted a wedge between them and they drifted apart early into the marriage. Careers and raising kids made things difficult too. But before all that Barid listened when she talked. At one time he was interested in her opinion. And that smile. He still had it but rarely showed it to her. It was a smile that could attract any woman; it drew her in.

The hot washcloth soothed her face. With closed eyes she pictured Barid stammering the first time he asked her out. He stumbled over words asking her to a frat party. She went with him, but it became clear she was uncomfortable so he took her to a pizza place where they talked for hours, closing the place down. Back then he opened doors, bought her gifts because she mentioned something once, and was excited about being with her. When exactly did it change?

The Barid she knew today was not the man she married. He used to laugh with her and even held her hand in public. None of the dreams and hopes for the future they talked about materialized. Other than the girls. They both wanted children, although he wanted boys. She was grateful to be blessed with girls.

She hung the face cloth on the towel rack and paused in front of the mirror. At one time they fantasized about travelling the world together. Now she worried about going a few hours away for a weekend. An audible sigh escaped her lips. Oh, how she loved him back then.

The front door opened. She glanced at the clock, 10:30. Before crawling into bed, she zipped up her suitcase and set it on the floor. Footsteps shuffled toward the bedroom. She felt him enter the room and rolled over to face him.

"I left your suitcase open in case you wanted to change anything I packed."

"Well hello to you too." He glanced at the bag, turned the suitcase over, dumping its contents on the floor, and repacked with clothes from his dresser.

When he closed the bathroom door, Jahana picked the clothes up off the floor, folded them and placed them in his wardrobe.

He returned to the bedroom, glanced at the floor, mumbled a thank-you and placed his zippered suitcase by the bedroom door.

"I'm looking forward to getting away. Thank you for planning this." Jahana waited for a response. Barid rolled over without a word.

Jahana lay staring at the ceiling, until her eyes adjusted to the shadows cast by the street light. What could she expect from this weekend away? If only they could slip into the people they used to be.

****

Mishal woke up early on Saturday morning, but couldn't make herself get out of bed even though she needed a head start on a busy day. *Just five more minutes.*

But thoughts of Jahana's text intruded on her quiet. Why wouldn't Jahana let it go? Now that someone responded to her, how long would it be until she explored her biological father's side of her family tree? Mishal would never encourage Jahana to seek out her father and his family, but she also wondered who he was. Aunt Noosha was a strong woman who wouldn't have a frivolous relationship. Any man she slept with would have been a significant part of her life. There would have been a good reason for her to bear his child. Jahana would come to the same conclusion eventually and look for him. Once that happened, Mishal feared, Jahana's family would never be the same. In fact, it was probably already too late. It never would be like it once was. If Mishal was in Jahana's situation, she would do the same thing to ensure her boys knew their ancestry. But from the outside looking in, it seemed to be the wrong approach. There were so many opportunities for things to turn out badly.

Mishal slid out of bed and stumbled to the washroom. The boys had soccer this morning and they would all need to be out of the house in the next hour. The boys stirred in their bunk beds. They loved soccer and would be downstairs before she was. Daydreaming put her behind schedule, so she pulled on her clothes and skipped the shower. Jahana's quest to find her mother's relatives consumed her too.

She reached the landing midway to the main floor when her phone vibrated in her pocket. It was a text from Jahana with the details of the hotel they would stay at in Quebec City. She preceded the details with 'just in case'. Jahana made sure her girls were her top priority.

She'd forgotten they were going away for the weekend. Jahana seemed apprehensive when they'd talked over their Friday coffee date. Mishal hoped Jahana's worry was for nothing. Perhaps this would be a new start for them. If they worked on their relationship, Jahana might not feel the need to pursue her ancestry. They'd talked about what she would tell him if he brought up the DNA test. It was a simple plan, but she hoped the topic didn't come up.

When she walked into the kitchen, all the cupboard doors were open, the boys searched for snacks to pack for the game.

"Okay, boys, sit down and eat some cereal. I'll get the snacks."

****

Cars crawled along the freeway. Jahana glanced at Barid. His clenched jaw told her to remain quiet. It was after three before they left because Barid worked late. She almost suggested they stay home, but didn't. An accident west of Montreal delayed them even more. Jahana breathed a sigh of relief when they opened the hotel door to a room overlooking the river.

"Room service seems like a good idea."

Jahana smiled. "That sounds perfect. This room's too beautiful not to enjoy."

She gazed out the window at the St. Lawrence River below, then glanced back at Barid who stood transfixed. Not on the river, not on the room, but on her or rather through her. She cocked her head, and he glanced away shaking his head. What was he thinking about? The moment passed, and he grabbed the phone, flipping open the room service menu. He ordered for them both, not bothering to ask what she wanted.

Jahana ran a bath and soaked until she heard Barid speaking to the bellboy. She wrapped herself in the robe hanging on the back of the door and joined Barid at the table off the living room. He'd ordered chicken cordon bleu and sparkling water for her. He cut into a thick steak.

"We are so lucky to have the means to enjoy a getaway, don't you think?" Barid raised his Perrier to his lips, peering at Jahana over the top of the glass.

"Yes, we are very lucky." Jahana swallowed. Was this going to deteriorate into an argument about how she didn't need to be working? She straightened and met his gaze.

Barid set his water down and lowered his eyes to his plate, cutting off another piece of well-done steak. "Do you think we should be contributing more to charity?"

"I don't know, Barid. You keep track of all the finances. Of course, if we can afford it, I would say we should."

"If we can afford this, then I think we can afford to help others." He held up a forkful of steak.

"Certainly." Jahana's shoulder's slumped. He had a way of making her feel guilty about things she didn't have any control over. It was his idea to spend money on a get-away, yet now she thought about many ways it could have been better spent. "Do you have any charities in mind."

Barid leaned back in his chair and cleared his throat. His legs stretched out under the table bumping up against Jahana's. A smile played at the corners of his mouth. "I have an idea or two."

Jahana waited for him to continue, but instead he brushed his toes against her bare leg and stared at her longingly. She stared down at her plate. It had been a long time since he had hinted at getting intimate. She swallowed a mouthful of water and raised her eyes to his. Half her chicken remained on her plate when he reached for her hand and led her to the bedroom.

****

Barid woke first.

"What do you say we have brunch here at the hotel, check out and do some sight-seeing before heading home?"

Jahana rolled over and faced him. "Sure." The luxurious pillows and feather filled duvet felt so inviting. She could have stayed in bed till checkout, but wanted to see something of the city before they left.

Barid rose and entered the bathroom. Jahana reached for her phone. There were several text messages from her baba. She sat up and opened them, heart pounding.

> *Where's the popcorn pan?*
> *Never mind found it.*
> *I'm letting the girls stay up late, hope that's okay.*
> *Glad you aren't responding, must be having a good time.*
> *Let me know you arrived, okay?*

Jahana flipped through her outgoing messages before responding.

> *Sorry Baba, thought I'd texted. Here safely. Beautiful room. See you later today.*

Jahana rose, put on the robe and wandered into the living room. Red maples lined the river, always the first to change color. Barid had fallen asleep quickly the night before. But she laid awake. He never worried about whether their love making satisfied her. She laid stiffly beside him, convincing herself that he wasn't about to change after this long. She needed to be grateful for what she had and quit thinking about what was missing. If only they were staying another night, maybe Barid would relax and they could slip into the versions of themselves they used to be. The bathroom door opened and Jahana returned to the bedroom.

Barid led her to art galleries and cute shops in the old city. He seemed on edge, like he had something to say. She knew there was no sense quizzing him about it. It would come out when and if he wanted to reveal it. Maybe she was misreading him. He didn't typically enjoy wandering through shops, so maybe that was why he was uptight. Jahana couldn't figure out why he was doing this for her. *Is he really trying to work on our marriage?*

They returned to the car. Jahana texted her baba to let him know they were on their way. She glanced at Barid. He gripped the steering wheel, a frown pasted on his face.

What had tipped him from a little on edge to stressed? "Thanks for the weekend. It was a lovely getaway."

Barid glanced at her before returning his gaze back to the road.

"You're welcome." Silence filled the car. Barid turned on the radio and scanned for an English station, turning it off and exhaling, his fingers tapping out his own rhythm on the steering wheel. He opened his mouth, then closed it again and stared straight ahead. Jahana leaned her head back and closed her eyes.

The hum of the engine and warmth of the sun streaming through the windshield lulled Jahana into a comfortable sleep. Barid's voice jolted her awake.

"I've been meaning to ask you something." Jahana's eyes opened, and she sat up straight glancing at Barid. This was it; he would ask about the DNA test. Jahana swallowed and looked straight ahead.

"There's a new woman at the office from Toronto, Muslim and knows no one in Ottawa. Do you think the two of you could get to know one another?"

Out of the corner of her eye Jahana saw Barid look at her before turning his attention back to traffic.

"Well, I guess."

Barid never asked her to do anything with his work colleagues. He rarely took her to work social events.

"What do you propose?"

"How about dinner at our place this week?"

Jahana noticed Barid's shoulders relax and one hand fell to his lap. Why was asking her to help a woman from his work so stressful for him?

"I'll ask her tomorrow." Barid smiled. "I'm glad you enjoyed the weekend."

Jahana leaned back and again closed her eyes. The fact he hadn't said he enjoyed the weekend gnawed at her. But he hadn't brought up the DNA test either. She'd call it even or in her favour. If they didn't talk about the test results after all this time together, she wouldn't worry about a conversation that would never happen.

They stopped for dinner and arrived home late. The girls were asleep and Barid popped into the office for an hour. Baba looked exhausted, but happy, when he headed out the door minutes after their arrival.

Jahana unpacked and threw a load in the laundry, then slipped downstairs to check on her MyGeneticFamily message board. The red flag showed one message awaited her. Was this finally a clue she could use?

The message was from someone named Miriam, who threw out some last names Jahana didn't recognize. Another dead end. She closed the message board and heard the garage door open as she climbed the stairs.

"Want some tea?"

Barid entered the kitchen, his smile reminding her of their dating years.

"That sounds perfect." He strode over to her, slipping an arm around her waist and kissing her on the cheek. Jahana stiffened and regretted it immediately. He pulled away.

"On second thought, I'll just head to bed." His footsteps retreated down the hall.

"Oh Barid, I'm sorry. Please stay and enjoy a cup with me."

Silence echoed down the hall.

Jahana settled at the kitchen table, sipping her tea, contemplating how life led her here. An idyllic childhood, married a man for love and had two wonderful daughters, yet she never felt so lonely. At this moment it appeared no one knew her true story. No one could tell her who she was. If only her maman was still alive.

She needed to ask her baba some direct questions, she'd run out of options. On her way to the bedroom she stopped at the girls' doors and peeked in. She had a lot to be grateful for and she needed to remember that. Barid's snoring drifted into the hall. She pushed open the door, the snoring continued.

As she slipped into bed, a floral sent caught her off guard. *Strange, Barid has a new cologne. I wonder when he started wearing it?* Her mind wandered to places she didn't want it to go. *No, we just had a lovely weekend together. I'd know if there was something more to worry about.*

****

Emad smiled, memories of the weekend rushing in warm and inviting. The board games, the snuggles, the movies, they'd packed a lot into a short time. The giggles took him back to Jahana's childhood. Where did the time go? He hoped the girls remembered the weekend fondly too. He understood the need to cherish the moment. As a parent, he thought there was lots of time. As a grandparent he realized time was short and unforgiving.

The weekend invigorated him. If he could keep this up, maybe he wouldn't need those antidepressants much longer. He sighed. For the first time in a long time he felt content, he had purpose again.

The phone interrupted his thoughts.

"Hello Baba. I just want to thank you for taking the girls this weekend they had a wonderful time and I hope you did too."

"Oh Jahni, it was a piece of heaven for me. Thank you for trusting me with them." For the first time it occurred to Emad she may have thought the girls were looking after him.

"Can't talk long, class starts soon, but I was wondering if you wanted to drop by the University for lunch on Thursday?"

Emad smiled. Not only was he helping her out with the girls, she was spending more time with him. She brought so much meaning to his life. "I'd love to."

****

The days flew by. Emad rose on Thursday morning. He considered taking the bus to the university, but the thought of someone, other than Noosha, sitting next to him again made up his mind. He'd drive. The cost for parking was worth not having to deal with the emotional fallout of another bus ride.

As it turned out traffic was slowed due to a fender bender. By the time he parked he realized he would be late getting to Jahana's office.

Just parked. Can I meet you in the cafeteria?

Of course. See you in a few minutes.

He saw Jahana immediately and settled in across the table from her. Her eyes melted his heart. The way she was quick to smile or reach out to comfort him. She had inherited many of her mother's mannerisms. She also adopted her mother's ability to get to the point. He had barely settled in when the inquisition began. Emad took a deep breath and chose his words carefully.

"It was a desperate time. Noosha was the youngest of three children born to Helen Kanooshki and Ardashir Jahakhana. Helen was of Russian aristocracy; some said a princess. Which, at least in my mind, makes you and your maman princesses too." Emad noticed Jahana's eyes roll. He knew she had heard all of this before, but he continued quickly before she could interrupt him. "Kamran and Nadim, her two brothers were much older. Following the revolution in 1979, Khomeini executed Nadim. We escaped two weeks prior to the execution." Emad shuddered. "Who knows what would have happened if we stayed."

Jahana shifted in her seat.

Before she could interrupt, Emad continued. "There was a lot of stress leading up to the execution and it caused Noosha to go into labour early. Complications resulted in the death of your twin, but you were strong and healthy." Emad touched Jahana's hand. "You have your maman's strength."

Jahana pursed her lips and lowered her gaze.

"We stayed to give your brother a proper burial and three weeks after you were born, we left Iran behind and came to Ottawa. Leaving your brother so soon after his burial was gut wrenching. If you weren't there to give us a reason to fight for our lives, I'm not sure we would have left."

Jahana's face softened. "Where did the rest of the family go again?"

"From what we understand Kamran, who married the Shah's daughter, immigrated to Switzerland. There are rumors your grandparents sought exile in the United States, but they may have joined Kamran in Switzerland. After Nadim's execution we lost contact with them."

"You've told me all of this before, Baba. Tell me something new."

Emad cleared his throat and wiped the corners of his mouth with his napkin. What could he say? There was so much he hoped she would never learn. He folded the napkin meticulously and laid it on his plate before taking a long slow drink of water. Raising his eyes to her, he licked his lips and began.

"There is something we kept from you. Just a year before you were born, your maman gave birth to another boy. Sadly, he too died during childbirth. The hospital was full, the doctors were busy and Noosha almost died too. At least your brothers aren't alone, they have each other."

"Why didn't you tell me about another brother before?"

"There was just so much sadness, and we didn't want to tell you another sadness from your past."

"What else is there?"

Jahana pushed back her chair and crossed her arms. Emad looked down. He couldn't tell her everything; she was better off not knowing.

Emad raised his head and swallowed. "Nothing Jahni. That's all there is." *Can she read my face?*

Jahana rose, looking at her watch. "I've got to go. Baba, I appreciate you telling me about your past. You and Maman had such difficult lives and I keep dredging it up, I'm so sorry. Please know I'm grateful for the life you gave me."

"And you are the world to me, Jahni. Without you, I don't know if we would have ever gotten over the pain. And now you're helping me get over another loss. You're my light, my joy, my reason for living."

He watched Jahana walk through the cafeteria doors and prayed she'd stop asking the hard questions.

CHAPTER ELEVEN

“I have to admit girls, I find the Valley of Independence and Attachment in the poem difficult to understand. Before I tell you what I think it is, do you have any ideas?”

“Does it mean we shouldn’t get attached to things?” Cyra scrunched up her nose and peered at Jahana.

“It could. How about you Sahba, what do you think?”

“I think the same as Cyra. You know how you make us clean out our rooms and give stuff to kids who don’t have as much as we do? Well I think it's about that. Giving up what you don't need."

"Good points girls. I also think it means fighting the urge to be comfortable and stop learning. Sometimes it seems easier not to try to be better, rather to sit back and enjoy what you have and not try to help others or better yourself."

Jahana swallowed. She was travelling through this difficult valley. It would be so much easier to put the DNA results aside and continue living the way she was. But she had to reach beyond wanting to keep things the same and discover where she came from. She needed to accept the changes in front of her and prepare herself for the disappointments that lay ahead.

"Maman." Cyra grabbed her arm and shook it. "Why does it say you can never get through this valley? Why try?"

"That does seem discouraging. But maybe it means there will always be choices in front of you and it is important to keep trying. Sometimes others will criticize you for your choices, but if they are made from your heart, they're the right choices for you. And yes, sometimes you might realize later you've made the wrong choice, but at the time it seemed right. I think it means that you can second guess your decisions and sometimes return to the decisions made and make a different one, but without making a decision, you'll never get through your situation. Life is full of decisions, so you never stop deciding and you need to forgive yourself when you wish you'd made a different choice."

"Or work towards making the choice a better one." Sahba stared at the ceiling.

"That's a good point Sahba. We need to be humble enough to admit when we've made bad choices. Getting through the Valley of Detachment with each decision relies on us wanting to make a decision, wanting to learn more."

Silence fell over the room. Her decision to discover her Jewish ancestry was the right decision. As painful as it might turn out to be. And she needed to keep asking the questions. Her baba might not like her asking questions he'd rather not answer, but she couldn't let that stop her.

CHAPTER TWELVE

M ishal tapped on the screen door and pulled it
open, cinnamon buns hijacking her senses. Her
parent's house did that to her. Echoes of her
childhood bounced off the dusty rose wallpaper.

"Hello?" The screen door swung closed and latched
behind her.

"What a wonderful surprise." Her maman appeared
around the corner like only a five-foot nothing wiry
mother can, an exuberant hug, warm and all-

encompassing. Mishal sighed and inhaled. *Why don't I do this more often?*

"You should keep your door locked." Mishal held her mother out at arms-length and momentarily met her eyes until she shrugged out of her grasp and pulled a hanger from the closet.

"Oh, pht." Hang up your jacket and come in."

Mishal did as her mother instructed and followed her into the kitchen.

"Come, sit down. Sit." Her maman pulled out a chair and motioned to Mishal who sat. No sense arguing.

"Baba, what's new in the world today?" He sat across from her; newspaper unfolded on the table, peering over the top of his glasses.

"Just the usual doom and gloom." His eyes settled on Mishal and he folded the paper keeping the creases exactly as they were when it arrived that morning.

Mishal's mother set a small plate in front of her and a large platter of cinnamon buns in the middle of the table. A coffee appeared, already prepared with cream and sugar, just the way she liked it.

"How is Adar? Have things settled down at school?" Baba leaned forward to take a bun from the plate.

Maman swatted his hand. "Let Mishal pick first."

"I was picking for her." Maman rolled her eyes and baba winked at her, pausing with his hand above the plate, while she picked the gooiest.

"He's doing well Baba. We're over the incident now. Seems like it's all behind him. He's still angry with me for bringing it up with the principal, but he'll get over it."

"That's good to hear."

Her maman settled in next to her at the table. "And, what's new with you these days? Do you see Jahana often? How is she doing? I've meant to get over and see her more but after your baba broke his ankle this fall; we haven't gone very far."

Mishal smiled. Her mother could string questions and information together like no one she knew. And it was the segue needed to lead into the questions weighing her down.

"Not too much new with me. Jahana's still having difficulties dealing with the loss of Aunt Noosha, but she's doing better. She regrets not knowing more about her mother's relatives, so I'm helping her dig into her past. Other than her maman's two brothers, one of which is dead, what else do you know? Are there any other relatives you're aware of? Any last names other than Jahakhana?" Mishal smiled to herself at the realization she may have inherited some of her mother's gift of run-on questions.

"Noosha never talked much about her family, but I remember one time she mentioned half brothers and sisters from a woman her baba married after her mother died."

Mishal leaned forward.

"Noosha assumed they moved to the United States at some point. She was grown when her baba remarried and had children with his much younger wife. Noosha said it was awkward to be around a step-mother almost the same age as her."

Mishal reached across for a second cinnamon bun, not wanting to interrupt. When her mother got on a roll, it was best to let her go.

"Noosha regretted not keeping in touch, but when the revolution threatened her family, she was grateful for the distance that allowed her to recreate herself and her small family and leave Tehran with no fanfare. Helen, that was Noosha's mother's name, had the maiden name Kanooshki and claimed to be of Russian aristocracy. Noosha thought those details were embellished, but she enjoyed her claim to be the daughter of a princess." Her maman stopped and lifted the cup of coffee to her lips.

Mishal took advantage of the pause to inject another question into the conversation. "Did Noosha's brother ever marry?"

"Now that you mention it, I believe he did. He was quite a bit older than Noosha and he had children too. But Noosha never said too much about them. The last name, Madani, rings a bell. I think she said the woman he married was a Madani."

Mishal took her phone out of her pocket and opened the notes app. Do you think that's spelled M-A-D-A-N-I?

"I would guess that would be the way to spell it. It's sad Noosha never spoke about her family to Jahana." Her maman took another sip of coffee.

Mishal eyed the plate of cinnamon buns, but decided to show restraint. The sugar buzz would hit soon, she didn't need to add to it. "I really don't understand it. Why wouldn't she look them up later in life. You know? You would think after twenty years or so she would start looking for her family."

Her baba who sat quietly across the table finally joined the conversation. "Maybe it was a case of trying to hide from who she was for so long, she didn't know how to bring it up later in life. And she'd lost track of the Jahakhanas."

Mishal nodded. "I supposed that's all there is to it. I just can't imagine not wanting to find you and Maman if we were separated." Mishal turned back to her mother. "I wonder if Jahana knows about the Madani name?"

Her maman shrugged and rose to check on the next batch of cinnamon buns." Mishal put her phone in her pocket and rose to place her cup in the sink.

"Stay, have another cup of coffee." Her maman grabbed the coffee pot, motioning for Mishal to sit back down.

"I'm sorry Maman, but I better get home, my house is a disaster. Thanks for the coffee and cinnamon buns." Mishal wrapped her arms around her maman and kissed her cheek.

"Just a minute I'll put some buns in a container for you to take home to the boys."

Mishal watched her maman dig through the Tupperware drawer for lids and then place the container in a bag after filling it with six buns.

"The boys will love this, thank you, Maman." Mishal hugged her mother again.

"Thanks for stopping by. Will we see you on the weekend?" She watched her mother pull the next batch of cinnamon buns out of the oven and place them on the top of the stove.

"I think so, I'll let you know." Mishal blew her baba a kiss on the way out the door. She pulled out her phone and texted the Madani name to Jahana who responded immediately.

Not a name on my list.

Something niggled in the back of Mishal's mind. Jahana's search seemed to get nowhere. And that was disturbing in more ways than one. That Jahakhana, a prominent Iranian name, hadn't surfaced in her DNA was troubling.

I hope she doesn't regret this.

****

Time to cast the net.

Jahana's tentative approach to the people who matched on MyGeneticFamily wasn't working. She composed a message to send to the remaining ninety-three matches.

> *I see we match as distant cousins. I'm looking for my mother's relatives. If you're familiar with the Jahakhana, Kanooshki or Madani surnames, please message me.*

The laptop balanced on her knees; feet rested on the coffee table. A cup of tea perched on the end table beside her. Barid left at the last minute on a trip to Chicago for the weekend. The girls were at sleepovers. The evening was hers.

A public profile on the site allowed anyone to see she had Jewish DNA. A Jewish woman wearing the hijab should intrigue most people.

After the ninety-third copy and paste, Jahana wandered into the kitchen and pulled out the popcorn pan. She'd watch a movie while she waited for responses. As the kernels popped, the phone rang. She glanced at it sitting on the counter; it was Barid. She let it ring out and called back a few minutes later. *Odd, he's not picking up?* She left a message apologizing for missing his call and asked him to call again.

She settled in front of the TV and flipped through Netflix. There were so many choices but none seemed appealing. When the phone rang, she jumped, forgetting she was waiting for Barid to return her call.

"Just got to my room. There's a snowstorm here, can you believe it? The flight was delayed, and it took forever for the taxi to get to the hotel. I wanted you to know I made it."

Jahana's brows furrowed, he rarely called on his business trips.

"Oh… okay thanks." What else was there to say?

An awkward pause followed. He seemed distracted. "Ah, well then. I'll call again tomorrow. Goodnight."

Before he hung up, a woman's voice pierced the background. "Barid what would…".

He was in the hotel room. Why would there be a woman calling his name? A random voice on TV wouldn't mention his name. Her thumb hesitated over the recall button. What would she say? Why would she call him back? Then she remembered something and hit redial.

Barid answered on the fourth ring sounding exasperated.

"Sorry if I disturbed you, but I remembered something I meant to ask you long ago. When we were coming back from Quebec City, you mentioned a Muslim woman from work you wanted me to meet. Is it something you're still planning? Did you invite her to dinner?" Jahana listened, but the room was quiet.

"Oh, sorry I meant to tell you. I asked her but she declined. Said she was too busy to meet anyone right now. I told her to let me know if she changed her mind."

Jahana listened beyond his response, but it was silent. The voice must have been her imagination. Barid would never cheat on her. Still an uneasy feeling stirred the pit of her stomach.

"Figured that must be the case. Sorry to bother you. Have a good evening." She listened until Barid hung up before disconnecting. In exasperation she tossed the remote on the coffee table, not feeling up to a movie after all. She picked up her laptop re-balancing it on her lap.

Five messages flagged from the MyGeneticFamily message box. Her heart quickened and she clicked on each message. They all said the same thing. No Jahakhana, Kanooshki or Madani names. How was it her matches were all dead ends?

CHAPTER THIRTEEN

"I've meant to tell you Mishal was over a while back and asked a lot of questions about Noosha's past. She said Jahana was looking into her ancestry. It's strange Mishal asked us. I assumed she'd talk to you." Silence fell over the other end of the phone.

Emad talked to his brother daily. They were close. His tongue suddenly felt oversized and dry. He took a sip of coffee to moisten his mouth and forced himself to swallow before speaking. "Jahana's having a hard time dealing with her grief. She thinks finding Noosha's relatives will help her. I'm not so sure. Noosha never contacted them or talked about them much and I don't think Jahana should either."

"Good point. Well, we had nothing to tell her, other than we'd heard the name Madani once? Anyway, I'm sure Jahana's filled you in on all this. I'll let you go. Call me if you want to go for coffee on Tuesday. Nice catching up with you."

Emad hung up the phone, his hands trembled.

Calm down. So, Jahana talked to Mishal about Noosha's ancestors. It doesn't mean she's gone ahead with the DNA testing. Emad took a deep breath. He couldn't keep ignoring the possibility any longer.

He grabbed his jacket from the hall closet and drove to Jahana's. When he pulled up to the house, he sat in his car contemplating what he was about to do. Before he lost his nerve, he stepped out of the car and marched up the steps and rang the bell.

As soon as he walked through the door, he realized his mistake. "Oh, I'm so sorry. I didn't realize what time it was. I'll come back tomorrow." Emad backed out of the doorway, tripping over the door jamb and catching the railing to stop himself from falling.

"Careful Baba." Jahana reached out to steady him. "Please stay. We just sat down to dinner. We have plenty." The girls joined Jahana at the door. Cyra grabbed his hand and pulled him back in.

"You can sit by me Babayi."

Emad slipped off his shoes and hung his jacket in the closet. By the time he reached the dining room, an extra place was waiting beside Cyra.

"Good evening Barid. My apologies for dropping in at dinner time. I wasn't thinking."

Barid smiled weakly. "No problem. You're always welcome at my table."

Emad took his seat next to Cyra. His stomach grumbled as he loaded his plate.

"You've been working and traveling a lot these days." Emad scooped rice onto his plate. The smell of Basmati making his mouth water. It bothered him how Barid was away from Jahana and the girls so much. One tenet of Islam stressed taking care of family. Many men interpreted that to mean earning a living to buy nice things. But Emad thought it was more about working on relationships.

"Yes, I've been busy with work. But it can't be helped." Barid bit into the corn on the cob and wiped the melted margarine off his chin with his napkin.

Emad turned his attention to the girls. Their excitement over the everyday things always made his day. He listened as they chattered about school and friends as he cleared the food from his plate. He was glad they talked him into staying.

Jahana opened the tub of chocolate swirl ice cream before he remembered his reason for coming over.

"Jahana, I was thinking the other day about that DNA Kit Barid bought you for your anniversary. Did you ever get tested?"

The ice cream scoop hovered in midair as Jahana, stared back at him. Emad glanced at Barid and noted his interest in the conversation too.

"Oh yes, I did. I didn't tell you because you weren't in favour of me doing it."

Emad caught Barid's smug smile telling him Jahana listened to him now.

"The results were weird; they didn't make much sense. No matches with names I recognized. I followed up with some of them to ask if the names Jahakhana, Kanooshki or Madani were familiar, but no one is related through Maman. They're all distant cousins, so perhaps cousins of yours Baba?" Jahana paused and looked directly at her baba. He glanced down at the table before returning her gaze.

"As I did the test to find Maman's relatives, I just gave up. I've had little time to pursue it. Now, who's having ice cream?"

Barid leaned back in his chair, seemingly satisfied with the information. But Emad was not. Jahana's quick dismissal of the topic told him there was more. He felt empty, gutted. How much of the puzzle had she put together?

"So, I've read that people get surprised by the ethnicity percentages. In fact, there's lots of controversy over the accuracy of them. Did your ethnicity come up as you expected?" Emad's stomach turned and he sat back in his chair, but kept his eyes on Jahana. He needed to know her reaction to this question.

Jahana looked at him. It was clear she wanted him to drop the topic, but the question hung suspended over the table. Emad's knuckles whitened as he clasped his hands tightly under the table. Barid interrupted before Jahana could say a word.

"What kind of question is that Emad? Of course, it would have shown her ethnicity to be Persian." Barid looked to Jahana for confirmation.

"There was nothing in that test you don't already know, Baba." Jahana's gaze bore through Emad. There was no doubt she knew about her Jewish ancestry and Barid did not. Emad's stomach turned. *Why did I ask that question in front of everyone?*

Jahana finished dishing up the ice cream and went into the kitchen mumbling something about being too full for ice cream. Emad heard her rinsing the dishes and stacking them in the dishwasher. He wanted with all his heart to go in the kitchen and hug her. Tell her everything. But he couldn't bring himself to do it. What if she hadn't found out everything? He expected she'd come to him when she was ready and he dreaded the day she found all the answers.

****

Jahana counted to a hundred and concentrated on her breathing. She rinsed the dishes so clean they didn't need the dishwasher, but still stacked and re-stacked them in the wire racks. She couldn't cry. No, she wouldn't cry. *Why would Baba do this?* She stood still, her hands in the dishwater, and stared out the window, not seeing beyond her thoughts. *Does Baba know? Why did he ask me those questions in front of Barid?*

"Jahana. I'm heading home." She jumped at the sound of her baba's voice, then shook her hands and wiped them on the hand towel before turning to face him. Sorrow revealed itself in his eyes. *I hope he can see the anger in mine.*

"Talk to you soon." Jahana raised her hand, struggling to smile. Her baba turned and strode to the door. Jahana couldn't bring herself to follow him. Her teeth clenched, and she turned back to the sink, reaching in and releasing the plug. The front door closed.

"Looks like I have to head back into work for a few hours. We're working on a proposal with a tight deadline. Don't wait up, I'll be late." Barid strode up behind Jahana and kissed her neck. She stiffened.

"Are you okay? You didn't join us for dessert?"

"Yeah, fine. Just have a headache that's all." She turned toward him, but he'd already left the room. Again, the front door closed. Noise from the TV wafted up from the basement. One stomp brought the girls up.

"No TV it's almost bedtime and you haven't done your homework."

"Awe, Maman."

Jahana wasn't in the mood. "Turn the TV off and go to your rooms. It's already late. No arguing."

The girls turned and retreated to the basement before stomping back upstairs to their rooms, slamming their doors.

Jahana sighed as she closed the dishwasher, programed it to start and glanced up the stairs. She should go talk to them, but instead she wandered down to her office.

Two new message notifications greeted her when she opened her MyGeneticFamily account. Had someone recognized her family names? She opened the message from Abbey Spitzer. Abbey was sorry to inform her she had none of those names in her family tree. The second message from Tarif Fassid gave a similar response. How could none of her matches be familiar with her mother's family names?

There had to be a clue hiding in her matches. She clicked on her DNA tab, then DNA Matches. A new match sat at the top of the list in a category she hadn't seen before: *Close Family*. The name, Sarah Abelman.

Jahana inhaled sharply. The confidence rating by MyGeneticFamily was extremely high. *What did 'close family' mean?* A quick Google query revealed Sarah was an aunt, niece, great-grandmother, double-first cousin or a half-sibling. Bile rose in Jahana's throat and the muscles in her jaw tightened. She rubbed her temples trying to defer the migraine spreading behind her eyes. When she clicked on the compare button, both profile pictures appeared side by side. She stared at a younger version of herself. Age probably ruled out the aunt and definitely ruled out the great-grandmother. Perhaps a double-first cousin, but the family resemblance was strong. Was she staring at a picture of a half-sister?

Was this person a link to her biological father? Jahana gasped for breath. *Okay slow down.* She closed her eyes and forced herself to breathe slowly. She hadn't seen this coming, although couldn't explain why. It was possible, in fact probable her biological father had other children.

Heat rose in her cheeks, and she alternated between clenching her fists and shaking her hands loose in mid-air. *Should I message her?* The curser hovered over the 'Send Message' button. What would she write? A frustrated growl escaped her lips. Best to leave it. Give herself some time to think about what she'd say. Jahana closed the message board and dragged her shaking legs upstairs, taking a deep breath before opening Cyra's door. She laid on the bed, reading and her gaze didn't shift when Jahana entered.

"I'm sorry I was so grumpy earlier." She slid in bed beside her daughter.

Cyra moved over, continuing to stare at her book.

"I love you. Sometimes mamans have hard days. And you knew you should do homework. Am I right?"

Cyra sighed and let her book drop, using a finger to keep from losing her place. "I'm sorry too Maman. We just wanted to watch the end of Survivor."

"How about we watch it together tomorrow night? I've got the PVR set up to tape it."

Cyra rolled into her arms.

"Now I better make sure your sister's in bed too." Jahana rose, placing Cyra's book face down on the nightstand, fumbling for the table lamp switch. "Love you bug."

"Love you too Maman." The words settled on Jahana's heart.

When she pushed open Sahba's door, her light was off and she laid in bed under the covers. Jahana crept over and smoothed her hair, leaning down to kiss her. She paused and whispered in her ear. "Sorry, love you little one." Sahba stirred, but didn't waken.

Jahana hesitated outside her own bedroom door. Should she go back to her office and write a message? She returned to the kitchen, turned out the lights and went to bed. *I'll sleep on it.*

I might have a younger sister. The thought rolled around in her head. All her life she wanted a sister, and the thought excited and frightened her at the same time. The closest she came to a sister was Mishal. *Until now?*

Jahana tossed and turned peeking at her alarm clock when the front door opened. It was one-thirty. One of these nights Barid wouldn't even bother to come home. He may as well sleep at the office. Before he reached the bedroom, Jahana rolled away from his side of the bed and feigned slow deep breathing. He was the last person she needed to talk to tonight.

The bedroom door hit the wall as it swung open. "Oh sorry." Barid whispered then flicked the light on in the ensuite and closed the door.

Could he be any louder? How was she supposed to pretend to be asleep through all of that? Barid fell into bed, tugging on the blankets.

She pulled them back. *Damn, she was supposed to be sleeping.*

"Sorry." Barid mumbled his apology again.

It was like he wanted her to wake up. She remained quiet, hoping he'd fall asleep.

"Are you awake?"

Jahana continued to inhale and exhale softly. His breathing slowed and turned to gurgles escaping rhythmically. She let out a sigh of relief. How could she talk to him tonight and pretend nothing changed when everything changed?

Barid's snores climbed up one side of her spine and down the other. at two-thirty-five she glanced at the clock. Would chamomile tea help? She sat up, hanging her legs over the side of the bed feeling for her slippers. Barid's rasps went undisturbed as she pulled the door closed and released the door knob.

Standing in the kitchen, waiting for the kettle to boil, thoughts of her sister continued to beckon her. The only way she would get any sleep was to compose a response. Even if she didn't send it. Just get the words out of her brain.

With tea in hand she shuffled down the stairs to her office and opened her MyGeneticFamily account. The icon showed a new message. She opened the tab. It was from Sarah. And it was long.

> *Hello Jahana,*
>
> *Have you been looking for me? I've been looking for you. Why is it I imagine people on the street to be you?*
>
> *When I was eight, I listened to my parents fight about a baby girl born before me. When I asked Ima the next day, she said I misheard. There was no baby. But I heard, and it's true. I've been sure I have an older sister somewhere ever since.*
>
> *When my cousin Adam had his DNA tested, you showed up as a cousin he didn't recognize. When you contacted him with names, he suspected you might be the sister I never knew. Adam and I are close and he knows how much I always wanted to find you. As soon as he showed me his results, I tested my DNA too. It took a long time for results, almost nine weeks but I couldn't believe my luck when I saw them. I don't know where to begin.*
>
> *I live in Israel with my Ima. I'm thirty-five years, not married, no babies…*

The message went on describing Sarah's life in Israel, Jahana skimmed as she tried to process what was in front of her. Sarah's parents had fights about her? Was Sarah's father ashamed of his fling with her mother? Did Sarah's mother forbid her to look for her?

When Jahana's eyes reached the bottom of the message, her hands flew to her mouth.

> *I remember hearing Ima say to Papa she felt like a piece of her was ripped from her body the day she left you at the orphanage.*

Jahana felt the blood leave her extremities, pooling in her torso, her knees weakened. Her stomach lurched. She staggered to the bathroom, dropped to the floor and vomited into the toilet. Her life was a lie. Neither of the people who raised her were her biological parents.

I'm adopted.

The bile swirled in the toilet and Jahana spit one more time, grabbing toilet paper to wipe the strand that hung from her bottom lip. She stared at her vomit, wondering if the lie hidden inside her made its escape. The line between truth and fiction was narrow. And now she crossed over to the truth because of one poorly worded sentence in a message from someone she didn't even know.

Another wave of nausea overcame her before it subsided. With knees pulled under her, she used the bathtub to hoist herself up off the floor. The cold water from the faucet and the fragrance of lavender soap soothed her. Sad eyes stared back from the cabinet mirror brimmed with pain at the realization her parents lied to her, her entire life.

She shuffled back to her office, shut down her laptop and climbed the two flights of stairs up to the bedroom. As she neared the door Barid's snores continued an annoying serenade. She entered and collapsed into bed, sleep overtaking her in a turmoil of images filled with angry faces and a father's disappointment.

****

"Time to get up, you'll be late." Barid rocked her shoulder. She opened one eye and saw him turn toward the door, already showered and dressed. Her other eye snapped open, and she saw the time. *Damn*. She grabbed her phone off the nightstand, unplugged it and texted Mishal.

Need to speak to you. Can I call you on my way to work?

The water barely had time to wash over her, Mishal's affirmative response spurring her on to hurry. The girls' argument floated down the hall. She didn't have time to referee today. She blew her hair dry and chose a yellow hijab to match the flowers in her blouse. She pinned it in place and checked her reflection before rushing out of the bedroom. The girls sat in the kitchen eating their cereal, tension hung in the air. Jahana chose to ignore the angst and simply kissed each girl on the top of their head, grabbed her lunch and headed out the door.

"Love you," she yelled as she pulled the door closed.

Too many words crashed around in her head and she needed a sounding board to absorb them. Someone to cut through the impossible and come up with a reasonable explanation for it all.

"Siri, call Mishal." Jahana backed out of the driveway. Mishal picked up on the first ring and Jahana didn't wait for niceties.

"Mishal, you won't believe this." Jahana blurted out the words, then paused. There was no way to ease into it. "I'm adopted."

Mishal gasped. Then a pause of silence before her voice recovered. "What? How do you know?"

"A new message showed up on MyGeneticFamily last night from a woman that matched as a close family member. She claims her mother left a baby at an orphanage and she's been looking for her sister her entire life." There was so much Jahana wanted to say, but paused giving Mishal time to process.

"That's impossible, Jahana. Why would your parents lie to you about being adopted? When Aunt Maryam and Uncle Ervin adopted their twins, we had a big celebration. I can't imagine why your parents wouldn't have celebrated too. It makes no sense."

Jahana took a deep breath. "But it all adds up. None of the cousins matching with me have any surnames I recognize in their family tree. I was blind thinking Maman must have had an affair. Clearly, neither of my parents are my biological parents." Jahana slammed on the brakes as the car in front of her suddenly stopped. Her fingers ached, and she loosened her grip on the steering wheel.

Mishal remained silent.

The car rolled ahead and Jahana inched forward. "Did you know? Why aren't you saying anything?" Jahana's heart pounded in her chest. It would be too much if Mishal was in on the secret.

"No, I swear. I'm just stunned. I don't know what to say."

The light changed and Jahana eased into the left lane, hoping it would move more quickly. She glanced at the clock. She was going to be late if she hit many more red lights. "Last night Baba asked me right in front of Barid and the kids whether I had my DNA tested?"

"Why would he do that if you're adopted, and he's been hiding that from you all these years?"

"I know, hey? Was I supposed to just blurt it out at the table in front of the girls and Barid? I'm so confused and lost. How can my entire life be a lie?" Jahana stepped on the gas and made it through the intersection on an orange light.

"Uncle Emad is smarter than you're giving him credit for. What if he asked his question in front of everyone because he was afraid you knew the truth? He could gauge your reaction without having you confront him, knowing you wouldn't say anything with an audience. In front of everyone was the safest place for him to ask. It must drive him crazy not knowing how much you know."

Jahana bit her lip and forced herself to breathe slowly.

Mishal continued. "Now let's be logical about this. You have a half-sister match that claims her mother gave up a baby. Do you know when she gave up the baby?"

"Kind of. She fled Tehran to Israel with her parents in 1979. If that's where she left the baby, it would fit perfectly into my parent's timeline."

"But that's it Jahana you don't know anything for sure. There are a lot of questions that need answers before you can leap to the conclusion Sarah's mother is your mother. Isn't it possible her father had an affair with your mother?"

"I hadn't thought of that. I guess because none of the matches have names I'm familiar with I leaped to the conclusion I'm adopted."

"There's more than one way you can be related to this half-sister. You need some answers. Do you think you can message her back and ask her where and when her mother had the baby?"

Jahana's heartbeat faded in her ears. Mishal was right, she needed to calm down and think about this reasonably. Was she going to take the word of a woman who overheard her parents arguing when she was a young girl? Sarah's mother might have given up a baby, but it doesn't mean it was her. There was still a slim chance her mother really was her mother. *How can I hope my mother had an affair?*

"Thank you for your voice of reason, you're right. I don't know what I'd do without you." A calmness fell over Jahana as she pulled into the parking lot. She'd managed to avoid any further red lights and she wasn't late. "Hey, remember that time we pricked our fingers to become blood sisters, because we said being cousins wasn't close enough to explain our relationship?" Jahana slid the gear shift into park and turned off the ignition.

Mishal's smile warmed her voice. "Well, we may not be cousins, but you'll always be my sister. DNA tests don't explain relationships. Remember that. No matter what comes of this, your baba loves you and I love you. DNA testing doesn't break those bonds. We will always be family."

"I know, Mishal."

But as Jahana strode to her office, she couldn't help considering how this DNA test made such a difference in her life. It would be difficult to carry on as if nothing changed, but she had to. Sarah's letter consumed her. When it came down to it, there were really only three facts. Her baba was not her father, she was half Jewish, and she had a half-sister. The rest of it was speculation. Noosha could still be her biological mother. Mishal was right. She needed to ask some difficult questions.

Jahana went through the motions of her day. Barid texted he wouldn't be home for dinner. *Good.* She watched Survivor with the girls and put them to bed. Deciding she needed some distance from the ancestry saga, she opted to avoid her computer. But as tired as she was, she couldn't bring herself to go to bed.

She sat in the living room flipping through channels, looking for something mindless and landed on a home buyers' show. It was about a Canadian couple looking for a home in, of all places, Jerusalem. She became immersed, studying every detail, the architecture, the landscape, the people on the street.

Jahana's head jerked as a key turned in the lock and the front door opened. She jumped up and greeted Barid. He hesitated when he saw her, closing the door behind him.

"You're up late. Did you wait up for me?"

"I'd like to say yes, but I was restless so watched something mindless to help me relax." Remembering her reaction to his touch in the kitchen the night before, she reached her arms around his neck and rested her head on his chest.

"Did you buy new cologne? I like it." She pulled back and searched his face for an answer.

"Oh, ah, yeah. There was a sale, and I decided it was time for a change. What are you watching?" Barid wandered into the living room.

"It's a house hunting show." The couple toured the Western Wall, a Jewish sacred site and tourist attraction in Jerusalem. Jahana watched Barid's expression. His brows knit and his head leaned to one side before his gaze landed on her.

"What kind of crap are you watching? Since when do you stay up late to learn about thieving Jews?" Jahana's bowels clenched, and she turned, picking up the remote off the coffee table.

"Oh, I was just flipping through channels and got absorbed in this show." Her mind raced and all she could think about was distancing herself from the possibility of being Jewish. "I'm not sure they're Jewish."

"Just what Palestine needs, more of their type."

Jahana turned off the TV. "It's just a stupid show. Let's go to bed."

Barid followed her up the stairs. She crawled into bed hoping he hadn't noticed her unsteadiness.

"Good night." The lack of sleep the last few nights caught up to her and allowed her to fall asleep quickly.

CHAPTER FOURTEEN

J ahana's hands hovered above the keyboard. Six days passed since she first read Sarah's message. Barid had been home for dinner every night since and the previous weekend they took the girls to Montreal on the train. Old Montreal's cobblestone streets and eccentric vendors helped take her mind off the drab November weather and the message she needed to write.

But it was Monday and Barid was back to working late. The girls were in bed and once again she sat in front of the computer looking at her inbox. She reread the message and prepared a response.

Dear Sarah,

> *Sorry I didn't respond sooner. I'm shocked to have a sister. I haven't been searching for you because I didn't know you existed. Until a few short months ago, I believed I was an only child of two loving parents. When results revealed I was half Jewish I questioned who I was. A cousin on my father's side also took the DNA test, and it turned out we weren't a match. This was a hard blow for me as not only was my closest cousin not my cousin, but this meant Baba was not my baba.*

> *As much as it was out of character for my mother, I believed she must have had an affair. Your message was the first indication the woman who raised me, and has now passed away, might not be my biological mother. It broke my heart and I'm not convinced, so I have a few questions for you.*

> *Where was the orphanage your mother left her baby? When did she leave the baby? And who is the father? Is there any chance she would take a DNA test?*

> *Growing up believing a twin brother died at birth has been my reality. Please understand, I'm excited at the prospect of having a sister, it's just taking me awhile to adjust to this possibility.*

> *I am Muslim and to learn half my blood is Jewish is a shock. Not that it bothers me, just that it may bother my husband and affect my children. My parents were very liberal, but my husband is more conservative and has Palestinian roots.*

I look forward to hearing more about you and the circumstances around my birth. Thank you for reaching out to me.

Salaam,

Jahana

Jahana reread the message several times and anguished over details. Should she say 'Salaam'? It was a very Muslim salutation. But that was what came natural. She hit the send button. There was no going back, she needed to find out who she was.

Scrolling through the DNA matches, she looked for a familiar name when another notification popped up indicating a new a message from Sarah. Jahana inhaled and clicked on it.

Dear Jahana,

Sorry to hear my contact is so disturbing for you. I can't imagine the shock you must feel.

I asked Ima all the questions you asked several times over the years, but she won't talk about it. When I told her I connected with you through DNA testing, she became angry. Please don't take this personally, she is kind and loving. This is not like her. Please be patient. I will ask if she will do the DNA test, but I doubt she will.

Ima left Tehran in 1979 with her parents. She was fifteen. Maybe an orphanage in Tehran, but don't know.

You are my only sibling.

I'll be in touch if I learn anything new.

Shalom,

Sarah

What's in a word? Shalom - salaam? Both words of peace and sound so similar. Yet coming from such opposing backgrounds. Warring factions that have at heart the same wish for peace.

> *Sarah,*
>
> *Thank you for a quick response. I will be patient as your mother works through something that is difficult. Is there any chance you could have misunderstood what you heard years ago? Could your father be the one who had a baby with my mother?*
>
> *I mean no disrespect by this inquiry. I just want to know for sure the woman I have loved all of my life was not my mother.*
>
> *Shalom and Salaam,*
>
> *Jahana*

Jahana waited for a response. But none came. Perhaps she pushed too far. She hoped she hadn't insulted Sarah. As Jahana was about to close out of her account, the new message icon caught her eye.

> *Jahana,*
>
> *Adam Samuelson is a cousin on my mother's side of the family. For him to be your cousin and mine, my mother is the link.*
>
> *Sorry. I know you must be sad to learn this. Wish I could hug you and let you know my love.*
>
> *Shalom and Salaam back to you,*
>
> *Sarah*

Jahana's body sagged. Tears pooled. She cleared her throat. Adam was the key.

It was like losing her mother all over again. She bit down on her fist, letting the searing pain distract her from the wail building inside.

****

"Siri, call Jahana's office." Mishal put the car in reverse and backed out of the parking stall, rubbing her hands on her pants trying to get the sticky punch off her fingers. Next time she'd volunteer for something other than punch bowl duty at the boys' gaming competition.

"It's killing me. Don't keep me in suspense any longer. What've you found out?" Mishal waited a week for an update, but couldn't wait any longer.

"I'm sorry I didn't contact you, but I found out last night and I'm devastated."

Mishal's heart sank. She changed lanes and pulled up to the light.

"Well, for starters, Sarah's mom left Tehran when she was fifteen years old, in 1979, the year I was born. Sarah pointed out our common cousin Adam Samuelson is her mom's nephew. This means she's my maman and I'm adopted."

Mishal heard the pain in Jahana's voice. What could she say? The light turned green, and a car honked.

Jahana continued. "Can you imagine, she was only two years older than Cyra when I was born?"

Mishal's breath caught. Cyra was a child. "Well, that explains why she had to give you up, she was too young to raise a baby. I'm so sorry. I can't imagine how you're feeling. It's a shock, but I want to remind you how much Aunt Noosha and Uncle Emad loved you. No matter the outcome of all of this, they're still your parents. Genetics aren't what makes a good parent, love is. And your parents had oodles of it."

There was a long pause before Jahana replied. "Oh, I'm grateful they took me in. But why lie about it? Why was it a secret?"

The same question nagged Mishal. "Does Sarah know who your father is?"

"It doesn't appear so. Her mother won't talk about me. She denies the conversation Sarah overheard. Denies my existence. And is furious Sarah took the DNA test and found me. My own mother wants nothing to do with me."

The click of Jahana's office door closing, followed by a sob carried through the phone.

"There's got to be more to this story. I'm sure Sarah's mother is trying to work through it all. She's likely worried you'll be angry? Can you imagine how difficult it would be to give up a child? Give her some time."

Jahana coughed and blew her nose. Mishal waited in silence.

"I need to be patient. But I'm hiding so much from Barid. First, I'm Jewish, then Baba isn't related and now neither is Maman. The secret keeps growing. Where will it end? I've asked Sarah to get her mom to take the DNA test, just to be sure, but she doubts her mother will do it."

"Are you going to tell your baba you know about your adoption?"

Jahana cleared her throat. "No, he's made such progress, getting out, socializing, dropping in to visit us. I don't want to set him back."

"You've opened a window to your past that didn't exist a few months ago. Give this woman space to adjust. And you too. Time has a way of working things through." Crappy advice but Mishal didn't know what else to say. She pulled the car into the driveway and waited for the garage door to open.

"Maybe you were a product of a first love, denied by her parents and you are the link to a man she lost touch with. What if you can bring them together?" It was the only positive spin Mishal could think of.

"I'm not sure I want to bring anyone together. Why didn't I listen to Baba? I should never have had my DNA tested. I can't unlearn any of this. It's like I'm losing my maman all over again." Fresh sobs escaped into the phone.

"Do you want me to come to your office?" Mishal rested her hand on the gear shift, sliding it into reverse. Jahana was the one who usually provided the voice of reason and comfort.

"No, no. I'll be fine. In fact, I need to get going. I have a staff meeting in ten minutes. I better get myself together. Thanks for the call. What would I do if I couldn't talk to you about this?"

Mishal moved the gear shift back up to park and turned off the ignition. *Do Maman and Baba know about this?* Had her parent's been in on it? Were they keeping the secret too? Adoption was accepted in her other cousin's families.

There had to be more to this.

****

"Baba, so nice to see you."

Emad noticed the guarded look in Jahana's eyes. Her hug was quick and light, not the usual heartfelt embrace.

151

The girls came down the hall, grabbing his hands and dragging him into the living room to play Wii bowling. Jahana didn't join them.

"Hey girls, I'll be right back. Just want to talk to your maman. Get warmed up."

Sahba grasped his hand. "No Babayi stay and play with us!"

Emad untangled her fingers, kissing the top of her head and breathing in the sweet smell of innocence. "You better get ready."

Pausing in the kitchen's doorway, he coughed. Jahana remained stooped over the dishwasher. He sauntered toward her.

"Jahni, I want to apologize for asking about the DNA test last week. Forgive me? Let's not let a DNA test come between us."

Jahana stiffened, but didn't turn to him. "There's nothing to forgive. I should have told you I was tested months ago."

Words came quick and sharp and her failure to face him, told Emad forgiveness was needed.

He touched her shoulder, and she turned. "Maybe I can help. Why don't you share the results and I'll help sort through the cousins?" His heart fluttered, not sure he wanted her to take him up on the offer.

Jahana's face remained tight, eyes emotionless. "There's nothing to see." She lowered her eyes and turned back to the dishwasher. "I deleted the account."

Emad's jaw dropped, and he clamped it shut again. "Why would you do that?" A tremor crept into his voice.

Jahana faced him, eyes blazing. "Because nothing of any consequence can come of it. I'll never find Maman's relatives."

Emad's mouth opened and closed before he returned to the living room. He played one game before telling the girls he had to leave.

"But Babayi, stay for dinner, please?"

Normally he couldn't resist their pleas, but today he needed to get out of the house to process Jahana's words. "Listen, I'll be back another day and spend more time with you." When he looked up Jahana appeared in the living room doorway, but didn't extend an invitation for dinner.

He looked back down at the girls. "I, uh, have to meet some fellas from my grief group this evening. We're meeting for dinner and a movie." Bile rose in his throat, the lie wreaking havoc with his stomach.

"So glad you have a group of new friends Baba." Jahana wiped her hands on a dishtowel, her tone quieter, apologetic.

"Yeah, me too." Emad turned to the girls. "See you two soon. If you want to beat your old babayi you better keep practicing!"

On the way home Emad contemplated Jahana's words. The ethnicity profile would show her Jewish ancestry. "Oh Noosha." His words rang hollow in the empty car, but he continued. "Did we do the right thing? Should we have told her the whole story? What's she keeping to herself? Why doesn't she ask about her Jewish genes? How much does she know? Did she really delete the account?" The silence of the car weighted the words. There was no one to talk to about this.

They had their reasons for keeping the adoption secret. Did Jahana give up before she learned too much? It was hard to gauge her reaction. How much did she know? The questioning had stopped. Was she at peace?

Emad pulled in front of his house and parked, a whisper of gratitude escaping his lips. "Thank you, God for guiding my Jahni. Please help her find peace."

****

The wind swept a few leaves from the corner between the fence and the house, swirling them skyward. Mishal shivered, the wind bit into her neck opening her unzipped jacket into a billowing kite.

"Hello Uncle Emad." She shouted over the wind gust as she raced from her car to the door held open just enough to welcome her but keep the leaves from swirling in.

"Hello dear niece. So nice of you to visit on this cold November day. The snow won't be long coming now."

They exchanged cheek kisses and pleasantries before Uncle Emad hung up her jacket and strolled into the kitchen.

"I've made tea, have a seat and I'll pour it before it gets too bitter."

Mishal perched herself on a chair at the table. The stained wood surface was no longer covered by a tablecloth. It would mortify Aunt Noosha he wasn't covering the blemishes. The house was neat and clean, but musty. The smell of a bachelor learning how to keep house. *It must be so hard living in the house he shared with the person he loved more than life itself.* It impressed her that he picked up the pieces and moved on.

154

Mishal noticed Emad used the Iranian tea set. Clear red glasses with worn gold gilt trimmings. She sipped tea from these cups many times over the years, but this was the first time she did it alone with Uncle Emad. He must have found it strange to find her here in his kitchen.

"I realized the other day that with the boys in school and winter settling in, I have more time to just pop in and visit. You must find it lonely in the winter when it's impossible to spend time outside."

Mishal hated making small talk, but she didn't quite know how to broach the subject she came to discuss. Hopefully it would weave itself into the conversation.

"It is lonely but hopefully this winter will be better than last. My grief group should help, we get together at least once a week." Emad settled into the chair across from her.

"That's wonderful. Are there any Muslims or Iranians in the group? People you might really connect with?" Mishal raised the red cup to her mouth and blew gently to cool the liquid.

"No Muslims or Iranians, but that suits me fine. I'm meeting people from other cultures. I prefer to socialize with a mix of people."

"Baba's much the same. Even after all these years he finds it hard to fit in outside the Muslim community though. I've an easier time, but Jahana struggles too. I suspect it's because she wears the hijab. People jump to conclusions when they see it."

Emad tilted his head, his brow furrowed. Mishal cleared her throat. She'd done a poor job at steering the conversation to Jahana.

"I suppose they do. Noosha and I raised her to be a strong woman. The hijab doesn't take that away from her, but I suspect it makes it more difficult. Far be it from me to interfere in her marriage though. If Barid and her agreed to certain more conservative Muslim ways, that's between them."

"Of course, it must be hard not to say anything though. You raised her to be liberal and a feminist." Mishal twisted her fingers in her lap and raised her head. Emad looked wistful. She let the silence hang, hoping he would continue to talk about Jahana.

"Jahana was so small, just a few weeks old when we arrived in Canada. We tried to teach her a few things about Iran, but we also wanted her to fit in here. And we were unhappy with how Khomeini was ruling the country. Like so many Iranians we tried to fit in, we didn't hang onto much of the Iranian culture. And Noosha was so afraid of being sought as a Jahakhana, we didn't even talk about Iran very much."

"It must have been very hard to leave behind so much of your culture."

Emad's eyes saddened. "It was, but the culture there had westernized a lot under the shah. And a lot of people were angry about that. We embraced the freedoms, so there was no place there for us when Khomeini came into power. And with Noosha's family being persecuted, we were grateful to leave it behind."

"Is there anything you regret about immigrating to Canada?"

Emad remained quiet for a moment then raised his head and looked into Mishal's eyes. "Noosha and I never regretted leaving, but we hoped one day Iran would have democratic elections, education opportunities for both girls and boys, and freedom to dress the way we want. We never thought we were leaving our sons behind in graves, never to visit again." Emad's voice grew husky. "Noosha never returned and that was one of her biggest fears when we left. I promised her we would return one day. We never did." He wiped his eyes with the back of his hand. His emotions were so real, she was sure there'd been deaths, but neither were Jahana's twin.

Mishal leaned across the table and placed her hand on his arm. "She's with them now, Uncle."

Emad cleared his throat. "Oh, I know she is. It's just funny how life has its own plans for you regardless of how you think it will turn out."

Mishal took a long swallow of her tea. "I'm so grateful you both brought your families to Canada. As a woman, I'm glad I wasn't raised in Iran. You and my father gave their girls so many more opportunities by coming to Canada. Is that what you were thinking when Jahana was born and you held her in your arms for the first time?" Mishal felt guilty continuing to probe, but she really wanted to find out more about Jahana's story.

A smile hinted at the corners of Emad's mouth. "I knew the minute I held her I had to get her out of Iran." The twinkle in his eyes faded. "There was no way I was going to raise her in a country that didn't respect people's right to practice whatever religion they chose."

"But Uncle, there's no problem practicing Islam in Iran."

157

Emad's face dropped and he looked down at his hands, twirling his tea cup. "That's true. But what about all the other people practicing religions? Like Jewish? How could I raise my daughter in a place that was so restrictive?"

Mishal studied Emad's face. In that moment she was sure he knew Jahana was Jewish. "I'm surprised lack of women's education wasn't your reason for leaving. Why were you so concerned about the mistreatment of the Jews?"

Emad sprang from the table. "Let me make another pot of tea." With his back to her, Emad replied. "Education was important to us, but the persecution of Noosha's family and friends who were Jewish were on my mind when I first looked down into Jahana's face." Emad paused and stared out the kitchen window.

"I didn't know you had Jewish friends. Were they business partners, neighbours?" Mishal leaned forward. Perhaps she was getting somewhere.

The kettle whistled and Emad refilled the teapot before turning to face her. "They were friends of a friend. No one we knew personally, but they had to flee the country or they would have been killed. We heard about it just that morning after Jahana was born. I looked into her eyes and vowed to protect her from such nonsense. I didn't want her living in a place where there was so much anger and fear."

Mishal sipped her tea in silence. It wasn't her place to question further. Yet she felt so close to learning something about Jahana's adoption. It felt like her Uncle Emad was struggling to hold it back. But this was Jahana's story. She wouldn't be the one to cause her uncle more grief. "Well, I know Jahana's very proud of her Canadian-Muslim heritage. And she's proud to be your child."

Mishal studied Emad's face. *Was there a glimmer of shame in his eyes? Have I gone too far?*

But Emad simply responded, "And Noosha and I've always been proud she's our daughter." Tears formed in the corners of his eyes.

"Oh, Uncle. I'm sorry my questions have upset you." She leaned forward and clasped his hand.

Emad placed his free hand on hers. "That's fine. Don't you worry. It's good for me to talk about these things."

Mishal glanced at the clock. "I'm afraid I need to go. I have to get groceries before I pick the boys up from school. Again, I'm sorry my questions upset you. I'm just curious about the past and your story is so interesting."

She rose from the table and placed her cup in the sink before reaching out to give her uncle a hug.

"I promise to visit more often. Take care Uncle." She stepped out into the frigid air, with more questions than she had answers to.

CHAPTER FIFTEEN

Jahana tried to see through the darkness to some sliver of understanding. It didn't matter how she looked at it, her adoption was a mystery. Why would her parents carry on such an extravagant lie for so many years? With the threat of the Khomeini regime on the Jahakhanas, she thought they'd be happy to announce her adoption, so everyone would know she wasn't a Jahakhana. In the Muslim faith, it was a bragging right to adopt. Yet, they pretended for all these years she was their blood and that she had a twin brother who died at birth. She always felt a little guilty about being the survivor, although her parents never made her feel that way. She lived and her brother died. Had she somehow caused his death? Used up all the nutrients in the womb so he couldn't thrive? She spent her lifetime in a quagmire of guilt about the death of a twin that never existed. At least now she could let that go.

Maybe if she learned more about her birth mother, she could understand and accept what she had learned to be the truth.

Once the girls were out of the house, she settled in front of her computer. First order of business was emailing her boss and colleagues to let them know she had no classes and would work from home. A day to herself would help her get some prep work done.

If she was going to the office, she'd still be driving, so she had time to compose an email to Sarah.

> *Dear Sarah,*
>
> *Not trying to rush you or your mom if you aren't ready, but I can't stop thinking about you. Would you be able to send me a photo and tell me all about the two of you? One day I hope we can meet.*
>
> *Salaam and Shalom,*
>
> *Jahana*

Composing a more detailed message tempted her, but she thought better to leave it wide open. Allow Sarah to tell her what she wanted her to know. Not inundate her with queries.

Throughout the day Jahana checked for new messages, but none came. By mid-afternoon Sarah was likely in bed in Jerusalem and so there was no need to keep checking.

Did she frighten her off? That seemed unlikely considering Sarah searched all her life for her. She was sure she would want to share stories with her.

The doorbell interrupted Jahana's thoughts, and she raced up the stairs and peaked out the living room curtains. Her baba stood on the doorstep, hands in his pockets, her heart stopped. What's wrong? Why would he be standing on the doorstep when she'd normally be at work?

She swung the door open wide, startling Emad.

"Baba, are you okay? Why are you here in the middle of the afternoon?"

"I'm fine, just fine." Emad waved off her worries. "I was driving by and saw your car out front so thought you must be home. Are you sick?"

"No, no, I worked from home today. Needed a change of scenery and to catch up on some things."

She breathed a sigh of relief; he was just lonely. "Come in."

"Oh no, I don't want to disturb you. Just wondered why you were home." Emad turned to leave.

"Nonsense, Baba. The girls will be home soon. Please come in, they'll be so happy you're here. Time for me to take a break anyway and I can use a cup of tea."

As Jahana plugged in the kettle and pulled down two cups from the cupboard, Emad settled in at the island. There seemed to be more to his visit than he was letting on, but she let him wrestle with it. They were still on awkward terms.

"Mishal came to visit the other day." Emad fidgeted; his chair creaked. "She was asking questions about Iran and our immigration."

Jahana stopped stirring her tea. "Oh, that sounds strange." She removed the teaspoon and set it on the saucer, raising the cup to her lips while keeping her gaze on him.

"It was nice to see her, she brought back a lot of memories. Things I'd forgotten about."

"Oh, like what?" Jahana's hand shook, so she set the cup down and placed her hands in her lap.

"Just how nice it was to cradle you in my arms. How hectic it was to immigrate with a newborn. How much joy you brought to our lives." Emad's focus returned from a faraway place to rest on Jahana. Her heart whimpered, and she cleared her throat.

"Oh, it must have been difficult." Jahana touched his hand.

"Babayi!" The door burst open and jackets and boots flew as the girls raced into the kitchen. "Are you staying for dinner?"

Jahana knew the conversation was over. Was he about to tell her something? She'd have to be patient.

"Baba if you don't mind entertaining these girls, I need to finish up my work for the day. You're welcome to stay for dinner."

The girls squealed with delight leaving him no choice but to join them in the living room while Jahana returned to her office.

Emad came close to telling Jahana the truth. Or at least most of the truth. The burden weighed heavy, and he was ready to talk about it, but he planned to be careful and find out how much she knew first. If he could carry the burden to his grave, he would.

"Thanks for playing with us Babayi. We've been practicing and we'll beat you this time." Cyra's top lip tightened across her teeth in the goofy grin he loved and she handed him the controller as his avatar appeared.

"Did your Maman practice with you?" Emad glanced at the girls before swinging and releasing his bowling ball on the screen.

"No, she's too busy. Maman makes dinner and after we eat goes to her office while we do our homework. She doesn't have time to play with us."

"Oh, that's too bad. I'll have to come over more often. I love spending time with you two." He reached over and tickled Sahba's foot, she squealed with delight

"That would be great!" Cyra wrapped her arms around his waist.

"Hey, no distracting the competition." Emad patted her back and winked at Sahba. "So, what's your Maman working on in her office?"

"I don't know but it seems to make her sad." Sahba peered up at him under her long eyelashes.

"Sad? How so?" Emad sat on the couch beside Sahba while Cyra took her turn on the Wii.

"I don't know, she seems sad all the time."

"Do you think your Maman's sad too Cyra?" Emad turned his attention to her as she completed her turn and returned to the chair.

"Yeah, but I think it's because Baba's never home, not because of the time she spends on the computer."

"Your baba's been very busy. You're probably right, I'm sure she misses having him around. One of these days his work will slow down and he'll be home more."

But Emad didn't think Jahana's sadness was because of Barid's absence. How much had she learned about her past? Why wouldn't she ask him questions?

"What do you say we make dinner for your Maman tonight?"

The girls leaped up and ran to the kitchen, rifling through the freezer until they found vegie burgers. Emad stepped out on the patio; the brisk autumn air blew the late autumn leaves he brushed off the barbecue propane tank into the neighbours yard. Sahba mixed a salad from a bag in the fridge and Cyra cut up fruit for dessert.

By the time Jahana emerged from the basement dinner was almost ready.

"What's been going on up here?"

Sahba grabbed her hand and led her to the table, already set.

"Dinner's almost ready, you sit and relax and we'll bring the food." Sahba marched out of the dining room and Emad settled into a chair across from Jahana.

"Thank you for this. They love having you here and so do I."

"My pleasure, I'm never happier than when I'm with you and the girls." A warmth spread through Emad. He contributed something to the family that afternoon, he was useful. A smile spread across his face.

Cyra and Sahba paraded in the food. After dinner the girls insisted Jahana relax in front of the TV while the three of them cleaned up. The girls went to their rooms to do homework, and he joined her in the living room.

"The girls worry about you."

Jahana's eyes narrowed. "How so?"

"They tell me you're sad and spend a lot of time on your computer in the basement."

Emad watched Jahana. Her eyes didn't sparkle like they used to, but then again, neither did his now that Noosha wasn't in his life. Jahana seemed distant and tired. Perhaps there was more going on in her marriage than Emad knew. Or maybe she knew all about the secret.

"Oh, just busy with work. I need to figure out how to better prioritize my time. I appreciate you coming over." Jahana rose and Emad took that as his cue to leave. It was almost eight o'clock and Barid wasn't home yet.

Jahana walked him to his car.

"Are you okay?" Emad stopped on the sidewalk and looked into her eyes.

Jahana rubbed her forearms and stomped her feet before nodding.

"Everything's fine Baba. Nothing for you to worry about." But her eyes lowered and told him otherwise. "Drive safely and thanks again for coming over and helping the girls make dinner. It was such a treat for me."

It wasn't his place to meddle. He climbed in the car and drove home.

****

"But how can everything be one?" Cyra rolled her eyes and flung her hands in the air. Jahana wished she hadn't insisted they read tonight. She thought it might bring Cyra out of her mood, but it seemed to exacerbate it instead. They read about the Valley of Unity.

"Think about a forest. We talk about a forest as one thing, yet there is so much inside a forest. Many individual trees, animals, plants and so much more. Yet if we can imagine flying high above the forest, it would look like one thing. Right?"

Cyra nodded.

"I know." Sahba propped herself on her elbow. "It's like the beach. When we grab a fistful of sand, we can see all the grains, but when we are walking up to it, it looks like one thing. Right Maman?"

"Exactly Sahba. When we look for differences and look closely enough, we see them. But if we stand back and look at the bigger picture, they all blend together and look the same. So, Cyra, what do you think the poem is saying then?"

"Obviously it's saying no one should be different, we should all think alike and become clones of one another." Cyra rolled her eyes again and let out a deep sigh.

"Remember how the last valley talked about understanding being different?"

Both girls nodded.

"Like the two of you, I find this vision of unity a bit hard to understand. I'm not saying you are wrong Cyra, because it might be your understanding. But I think of it as looking at everyone as one of God's children. If we could look at each other that way, we could put aside jealousy and anger and pride and instead work towards a common goal of love. There's a little more to it as well, but I don't want to give away the ending of the poem."

Cyra rolled off the bed. "Can I go to my room?"

"Yes, I'll come see you in a few minutes."

Sahba rolled off the other side, pausing before leaving. "I like it when you read to us Maman."

"I like it too Sahba."

Jahana lay on the bed listening to the girls get ready for bed. The weight of knowing her baba wasn't her biological father took its toll. *I wonder if Cyra can feel it?* And yet, here she was telling the girls to see similarities and think of themselves as part of a larger picture. If she truly believed that, she wouldn't worry about finding out more about her mother's family and figuring out where her Jewish genes came from. What did it matter? Was it really going to change who she was?

Stand back. Look at the bigger picture. Maybe she needed to let it all go.

CHAPTER SIXTEEN

Mishal set down her casserole on the kitchen counter before kissing her maman's cheeks and embracing briefly. The boys wrestled with their babayi in the living room. Hamid refereed to ensure everyone's safety.

"The chicken smells so good Maman, I'll just slip my casserole in the oven to finish cooking." Mishal opened the oven door and placed her potato casserole next to the roasting chicken. "Now what can I help with?"

And so, another Sunday dinner unfolded as it always did. Men socializing, women working. Mishal gazed out the kitchen window. Large wet snowflakes floated to the ground some lingering in the stunted green grass hanging onto the last glimmer of summer color.

"Okay boys, dinner time. Wash up." The boys sweaty and wound up took their places at the table. Mishal listened to the conversation revolving around school and soccer. She glanced around the table and noted all the things she was grateful for. A wonderful husband, healthy boys and parents who wanted to be part of their lives. Jahana would never enjoy another family dinner with Aunt Noosha.

"Did you hear that the new neighbours just adopted a baby boy?"

Mishal stared in disbelief at her mother. Had she really just brought up adoption? "That's exciting. How old is the baby?"

"Just a few weeks old. I guess they arranged it prior to the birth. Not a surrogate, but a young woman who couldn't keep the baby, known by a cousin to them."

"That's so exciting. I'm glad it worked out for them. It must be hard as a parent to decide whether to tell your child they're adopted." Mishal rested her fork on her plate and looked from one parent to the other, trying to gauge their reaction.

"Oh, there's no choice. Tell the child. It's best to always be truthful about it. Can you pass the potatoes please?"

Mishal passed the bowl to her baba. "So, is there ever a time when the child shouldn't be told?"

Her baba took another scoop of potatoes and set them down next to his plate. "I can't think of one, can you?" He glanced up at Mishal.

"No, but there're a lot of parents who don't seem to."

"It's been my experience Christians seem to be more comfortable hiding the truth about adoption than Muslims."

Mishal took a quick sip of water. "Why do you say that Baba?"

"I don't understand hiding such an important fact from a child, and I don't know any Muslims who haven't told their children."

For a moment, time froze. Her mother, nodded as she raised another fork to her mouth. If her parents knew of Jahana's adoption, they didn't show it. Her baba and Uncle Emad were close. He helped Uncle Emad and his family immigrate to Canada. She thought they knew everything about each other. How could there be family secrets between them? When would the lies and secrets end? All of this mystery over an adoption? But why?

The usual post Sunday dinner rituals fell into place. Her baba dozed on the couch. Her maman worked on the latest knitting project. The boys sat watching a movie and Hamid read the paper. Mishal observed the scene in front of her with new eyes. So much was not what it appeared. How many secrets were there?

****

Jahana slid through her maman's grip, eddies of frigid air twisting her tiny body in a vortex until the ground rose to meet her.

"Maman!" A silent scream caught in her throat delivering her out of a dream. Sweat trickled down her neck.

Jahana's breathing slowed, but the nightmare remained vivid. She padded to the bathroom, sat on the toilet seat, and fell apart. Tears drenched her cheeks; her hand covered her mouth to quiet the sobs. Her maman's eyes haunted her as she held her at arm's length over the cliff's edge; affectionate, then amused, and cold. Blue lips said something before a vapor rolled between them. Jahana shuddered.

Why was her maman coming to her now? And in such a horrible way? Was her spirit reaching out from the grave to tell her something? Was she upset Jahana uncovered the secret? Or was she letting her go to pursue the truth?

The bed creaked and Jahana dabbed her eyes with a wad of toilet paper, throwing it in the bowl before returning to bed and skimming between the sheets still damp with sweat. A shiver escaped through clenched teeth before she pulled the duvet up to her chin, the blanket trapping her body warmth. The clock blinked 4:58, she'd wait for Barid's alarm.

Barid showered and lingered in the bedroom. It wasn't like him to hang around until she woke and she wondered what was on his mind. She swung her legs over the side of the bed and started for the bathroom. Barid picked up a coin off his dresser and slipped it in his pocket.

"Ah Jahana, I was hoping to catch you. I've invited that Muslim woman from work to dinner Sunday evening."

Jahana stopped and turned to him. "Oh, what time?"

"I told her 6:30?" Barid looked like a schoolboy awaiting approval, his hand still lingering in his pocket. Excitement and expectation written across his face.

"Ok. What's her name?" Jahana stepped into the bathroom, turning back toward Barid.

"Maha." Barid smiled.

"Can't wait to meet her." Jahana tried to sound enthusiastic, but she was tired and really needed no further distractions in her life. She stopped herself. This woman likely needed another woman to talk to, and she wasn't too busy to help her out.

Barid popped into the bathroom and kissed Jahana on the cheek. "I think you'll really like her." His eyes shone with excitement. Jahana shook her head as he left the bedroom. She gave up trying to figure him out long ago.

She arrived at work early, so checked her MyGeneticFamily inbox. No new messages, but there was a new match. *What now?*

Under the heading of 'Parent/Child' appeared a grey female silhouette and the identity hlsi231. Jahana felt the blood drain from her extremities, palms cold and clammy. She closed her eyes and calmed her breathing. This day, this moment, surreal. It was a far cry from her reaction to learning she was Jewish.

Jahana wanted the truth and here it was staring her in the face. She opened the message board and typed. She'd wasted enough time.

> *Dear hlsi231,*
>
> *Addressing my birth mother by random letters and numbers, is not how I pictured our first communication, but it appears this is how you want me to know you.*

I've lived my life ignorant of who I am: that I am adopted, that the two people I knew as my parents do not share the same genes. I'd never ask more of you than you can give, but I implore you to tell me about yourself, about me, about where I come from.

I want to know my story and how I was once part of yours.

Jahana

Jahana sent the message without re-reading. There'd been too many people thinking twice before relaying messages in her lifetime. The truth was close, time to reveal the secret and deal with the consequences.

CHAPTER SEVENTEEN

Emad accompanied Jahana to her Saturday morning volunteer session with the immigrants. She'd asked him to help her out because there were so many participants. While driving to the class, Emad talked to Jahana about the girls' concerns. It was one of the few times the two of them were ever alone. He hoped there was enough time to get to the bottom of things.

The air was crisp and the sun shone, although low on the horizon as it always was this time of year. This would be the last session until the new year as the centre closed down for the Christmas holiday.

"When I was at your place the other night, the girls were telling me that they think you're sad. I'm worried about you Jahni. Are you okay? Is there something wrong?"

"You already told me that. I've been pre-occupied with work, that's all."

"They also said Barid is rarely home. Far be it for me to interfere, but is everything okay with your marriage?" Emad held his breath and looked out the side window.

"They're right about Barid working lots of overtime. I know over the years work has had its ebbs and flows, but he has really gotten into the habit of working late. I don't ask him about it. I just keep hoping it will end soon. I know it affects the girls and I feel really badly about that. I guess maybe it's affecting me too."

"The girls say you're also spending a lot of time in your office on your computer. I thought this semester was going to be an easier one for you?"

"It has been easier. I've just been working on a special project. I hadn't realized it was affecting the girls so much. Thank you for letting me know. I'll make an effort to spend more time with them."

"And the sadness. Are you sad? Is it your marriage or something else?"

Jahana paused before responding to the question. He felt badly asking as he had always made a point of not interfering or asking about her relationship with Barid. He knew she used to confide in marriage tribulations with Noosha. Now that she didn't have her mother to talk to, maybe she would appreciate his attempt to talk with her.

"I suppose Barid's absence has had an effect on me too. That's probably what the girls are sensing. I do worry about him working so much and ignoring his family. But I also know what it's like to have too many things to get done at work and not enough time. I'll talk to him about it. Especially now that I know it is bothering the girls so much too."

Jahana pulled up in front of the community centre. Ridges of snow lined the sidewalk making it difficult to park.

"I'm sorry Baba, but it looks like I'll be parking beside a snowbank."

Emad wiped the humidity from the side window and peered out. "No problem, I'll manage."

Parking spots were at a premium and this one was close to the community centre. He was just thankful someone shoveled the walks. The night before he listened to the blizzard howling outside his window and worried they'd be trudging through snow for blocks. It seemed he worried about too many things these days, things that didn't need his worry.

The door barely cleared the snowbank, and he surveyed his path to the sidewalk. A tentative step revealed he would sink to his knees. Then Jahana was in front of him, offering her arm. Not that long ago he was the one helping her, carrying her over snowbanks. Where had the time gone? Using her arm to steady himself, he navigated his way over the wall of snow. He gave her arm a squeeze and she turned to him.

"Are you sure there's nothing else?"

The girls were right, Jahana's eyes did hold a sadness that had never been there before. He could see it amplified as she turned towards him and smiled.

"That's all Baba. No need to worry about me."

But Emad did worry. There was something he was sure she was hiding behind her calm exterior. The hair on his neck prickled as he thought about what it could be.

****

Jahana prepared lamb stew for Sunday dinner. Barid spent the entire weekend at home for a change and the girls didn't let him out of their sight. She wished Maha wasn't coming to intrude on it.

The doorbell rang and Barid jumped up, composing himself before opening the door.

"As-Salamu-Alaikum." Maha bowed.

"Wa Alaikum Assalam wa Rahmatullahi." Barid placed his hand on his heart, bowing in return, welcoming her into the house with a sweeping gesture, stumbling over his own feet as he closed the door. "My wife Jahana and our daughters Cyra and Sahba."

"As-Salamu-Alaikum." Jahana stepped forward. "Please come in. Let me take your coat."

Maha quickly removed her jacket and handed it to Jahana.

"Please go in."

Barid led her to the sitting room and Jahana followed behind.

"Please sit wherever you like."

Maha chose the end of the loveseat, hands resting in her lap, gaze lowered.

Jahana expected an older woman, but she was probably ten years her junior. Or maybe she just appeared younger because she was so tiny. And the hijab made it harder to tell how young she was.

"Can I get you something to drink? Juice, water?"

"Water would be nice. Thank you." Her response was quiet, her eyes never rising to meet Jahana's.

"Barid, what can I get you?"

"Oh, orange juice would be great. Thank you." Jahana escaped and took her time, stopping in the living room where the girls watched a movie.

With two glasses of water and an orange juice on her maman's gold gilded serving tray, she approached the sitting room. Barid's laughter extended down the hallway. When she entered the room, Maha's smile disappeared, and she stood to take the glass from Jahana.

"So Barid tells me you're an executive assistant for Peter. How long have you been doing executive assistant work?" Jahana leaned in to hear her answer.

"This is my fifth year."

Her voice was low, and it took Jahana a few seconds to interpret the words she muttered.

"Oh, you look so young, I thought perhaps this was your first job." Barid scowled at her. "I mean you have great genes." Jahana cleared her throat. "I'm sorry, please excuse me. I need to check on dinner." Jahana's face burned.

What's the matter with me? Barid's chuckles followed her into the kitchen. *Why do I feel so awkward around this woman?*

Jahana called the girls to help get dinner on the table. Cyra and Sahba carried the conversation talking about school, piano lessons and the latest books they were reading. Maha politely listened, although remained awkwardly quiet. Jahana found it surprising she accepted Barid's dinner invitation.

"What made you move to Ottawa?"

Barid shot her a look, but it was too late. The question hung over the table.

Maha laid her fork on her plate and for the first time met Jahana's eyes. "Two years ago, my husband died in a car accident. I wanted to find a smaller city to raise our son."

For the second time that evening Jahana's face flushed. "Oh, I'm so sorry, I didn't know." She widened her eyes in Barid's direction. His glare showed his displeasure. "I wish I'd known you had a son. You should have brought him too."

Maha's sad eyes lingered on Sahba and Cyra and she forced a smile. "That's kind of you, but my son lives with my parents in Toronto. Once I'm settled, he'll live with me here."

It was more than Jahana could stand. Why hadn't Barid filled her in on these details? "Oh, next time then."

"Girls why don't you tell Maha about the science fair." Barid's interjection was the first thing he'd done right since Maha arrived.

Jahana pushed her carrots around on her plate while Cyra and Sahba discussed their projects.

After dinner, the girls returned to the living room to finish their movie.

"Jahana," Barid addressed her tentatively. "I've told Maha we'll help her out. She's found an apartment two blocks over. Until she gets on her feet, I've offered to pay her rent."

Jahana looked from Maha to Barid and back again. Why was he bringing this up now? He could have told her this before she arrived.

"Oh, well..." She pasted a smile on her face, not knowing what else to say.

Maha glanced up before returning her gaze to the tablecloth.

"It will be our pleasure." Jahana finished.

Maha raised her stare and with pleading eyes looked through Jahana. "I appreciate the help and generosity."

"Perhaps you can help Maha get settled in her new place? She'll be moving early January."

"Certainly," Jahana turned her attention from Barid to Maha. "What can I help you with?"

"Oh, that's kind, but my parents will come help the day the moving truck arrives from Toronto. I'm staying in a furnished place here so won't have anything to move out of there." Maha shifted in her chair. "I appreciate the offer though."

"I'll make myself available that day." Barid smiled, his eyes softening. Jahana glared across the room at him. He barely had time for his own family, how was he finding time for her?

"I appreciate dinner. Can I help you clean up?" Maha looked into the kitchen. Piles of dishes covered the counters.

"Oh, no the girls will help."

"Well then, if you don't mind, I'll call a taxi. I've taken up enough of your evening." Maha removed a phone from her pocket.

"No, no, don't be silly. I'll drive you home." Barid pushed his chair away from the table.

Maha smiled. "So, kind of you."

Jahana cleared up alone after dinner glad for some time to herself. Once the girls were in bed, she poured herself a cup of tea. Barid texted to say he was stopping at work to take care of a few things, he'd be late. Jahana waited up.

The sound of a key in the front door startled her, and she glanced at her phone. It was almost midnight. She waited for Barid to walk down the hall before calling out to him. "Maha get home?"

Barid peered into the darkened living room, reaching for the light switch. "Of course. What kind of question is that?"

"I think we both know. What's going on with Maha? Why did you really bring her to meet us?"

Barid moved to the couch beside her. She slid over and swung her feet up between them, a scream building inside her. She forced herself to leave the silence for him to fill.

"Like I told you, I just wanted her to meet you. She knows no one, and I thought you could be friends."

Jahana stared at him, refusing to give him the satisfaction of a response.

"Jahana, it's my duty as a Muslim man who makes a good wage to share with the less fortunate. She needs someone to help her out."

So, this was how he would spin it. Make himself out to be some sort of hero. "But there's more to it isn't there? I'm not stupid Barid. Although I realize just how stupid I've been."

Barid cleared his throat and took a deep breath. "I'm not sure what you're getting at. It's late. Let's go to bed." Barid rose from the couch, but Jahana didn't move.

"Exactly what have you been doing for her?" Jahana's voice trembled.

Barid sat back down. "Now Jahana, it's the duty of a Muslim man to help a woman left without male support. I feel very obligated to do what I can. This isn't how I wanted to bring this up, but since you seem to have figured it out, I might as well tell you, I plan to take Maha as a second wife."

Jahana's eyes widened and jaw dropped.

"This is something I've been thinking about for a few months and you know Islam allows it."

Jahana reacted with vehemence, tossing the rest of her cold tea in his face and swinging her legs over the side of the couch.

He grabbed her arm and pulled her back down. "I understand you're upset, but helping the less fortunate is a tenet of Islam." His eyes blazed righteously.

Jahana glared at him, then lowered her gaze to his white knuckles squeezing her arm. His grip released, and she shook free. "As I understand the laws of Islam, I don't have to accept this situation."

"But you will for the sake of the children." Barid growled the words at her.

Jahana rose and strode out of the room, her maman's voice echoed in her head. *You are strong.*

She heard the front door close. Barid never came to bed.

****

Mishal maneuvered her way through the crowded halls, stale air permeating her senses. When she walked through the cafeteria doors, she spotted Jahana already seated in the back, waiting. Mishal glanced at her phone; she was early. She'd guessed this was serious. Jahana never called on a Monday asking to meet for lunch. The label of Jahana's water bottle lay in tatters on the table. Mishal swallowed and pasted on a smile.

"Hello cousin." Mishal leaned down and kissed Jahana's cheek, then held her shoulders, inspecting her eyes before taking her seat.

"Not sure calling me cousin is appropriate anymore."

Mishal pursed her lips. "You will always be my cousin. Now what's up. What's put you in this mood?"

Tears pooled in Jahana's eyes.

"Oh, no, what is it? What have you found out?"

"Oh, it has nothing to do with my DNA." Jahana sighed. "It's Barid."

Barid?

Jahana struggled, opening and closing her mouth, trying to find the words, throwing her hands up and blurting out a simple sentence.

"He wants to take on a second wife."

Mishal's eyes widened, and she sat forward grasping Jahana's hand. "What? Is that what he said?"

"Yes, he was very clear."

"But it's not legal in Canada."

"It's not, but it happens all the time." Jahana's voice shook and Mishal felt the tremor in her hand. "There are Imam's who perform second, third and even fourth marriages in their mosque. It's done in Toronto by a few Imams. In fact, I should consider myself lucky as apparently some of these Imams counsel men not to tell their current wives about subsequent wives. At least Barid had the decency to tell me and seek my approval."

"So how do they justify it when it's illegal?" Mishal searched Jahana's face, horrified at what she was telling her.

"Since it's sanctioned by Islamic law, some feel that supersedes Canadian law. Other's feel differently and believe Canadian law supersedes Islamic law. I have read it described by those who don't support it as a 'halal affair' and I have to say I agree with them. In my opinion it's nothing more than an Islam approved mistress. It's interpreting Islam in a way I don't support." Jahana inhaled deeply, her cheeks flushed.

Mishal paused before responding. "Of course, you can't support it. It's archaic and a slap in the face. Consider your girls, they can't grow up thinking this is acceptable. You need to refuse to be a part of this."

Jahana shuddered. "It's a nightmare. If I refuse, he may choose her."

"Divorce is an option. Islam states a wife needs to agree and may divorce if she doesn't agree."

"I know, but I feel so guilty. This is a widow with a small child. Am I selfish not wanting to share my husband to help her out?"

"He can help her out without sleeping with her." Mishal clamped a hand over her mouth. She didn't mean to be so blunt. When Jahana didn't react, she continued. "He's choosing this woman over you and the girls. Fault falls on his shoulders."

"But I must not have been enough. Could I have done better? Should I have?" A tear slid down Jahana's cheek and she wiped it away with the back of her hand.

"Again, this is not your fault. He's not the man you married. He used charm and acceptance to get you to marry him."

Jahana covered her face with her hands.

Mishal touched her arm and stroked it. "He keeps changing the rules. You've accommodated his wishes. But this is going too far don't you think?" Mishal gripped her arm reassuringly.

"I do," Jahana whispered. A smile tugged at the corners of her mouth. "Rather an appropriate response, don't you think?"

Mishal sighed. "Yes, I'd say it's a very appropriate response.

"I'll talk to Barid tonight and make sure I understand his intentions and I need to know how long he's been carrying on a relationship behind my back." Jahana straightened in her chair as she talked. "I'll try to reason with him about what this means for us and for the girls. He needs to understand I can't agree to this."

THE LIE

Mishal squeezed Jahana's hand. "You're a strong woman. If there's anything I can do, let me know."

Jahana squeezed her hand back, then glanced at her phone. "Oh no, I'm late. Do I look okay?"

Mishal rubbed some smeared mascara off her cheek and smiled. "You look fabulous."

The minute Jahana walked away, Mishal's fists clenched. *That bastard. He doesn't deserve Jahana or his daughters.* He was the source of all the ugly in Jahana's life.

Mishal rose and made her way to the car. She too thought him charming when Jahana dated him. She shook her head, grateful that her husband remained true to the person he was before they married. It wasn't just the hijab that bothered Mishal, it was how he tried to isolate her. Jahana was too strong for that. She kept family close, although she didn't seem to have many friends.

This time, he'd pushed too far.

****

Emad called and left messages for two days, but Jahana didn't respond, not even to texts. By Tuesday afternoon, he could wait no longer. Parking in front of Jahana's house he noted the front walk trampled into a barely usable path. No one had shoveled after the snowstorm the day before. A yellow shovel poked out of a snowdrift to the right of the front steps so he exited the car and retrieved it.

When Jahana pulled up, her finger wagged in his direction before the car stopped. He paused and wiped the sweat from his brow.

"Baba, you shouldn't be doing that. Barid will do it this evening."

"Oh, it's good for me. Nice to get a little sunshine on a winter's day."

Jahana's face appeared drawn and her shoulders slumped under an invisible weight. Something happened since he last saw her. He was right to worry.

"Put down that shovel and come in. I'll make you a warm cup of tea."

Emad followed Jahana into the empty house.

"Please excuse the mess." Jahana filled the kettle and tidied as it warmed.

Emad stacked the breakfast dishes still on the counter and Jahana rinsed dinner dishes from the night before, placing them in the dishwasher. This wasn't like Jahana at all. She was particular about her kitchen. He'd never seen it in such disarray.

Jahana pulled down china teacups from the overhead cupboard. They'd been Noosha's cups. Emad noticed the dark lines under her puffy eyes. There was definitely something wrong.

"You worry me, Jahni. You haven't returned my calls or my texts. Has something happened?" Emad settled in at the island.

"Oh Baba, Barid's been working so much I've barely seen him. I'm just tired from carrying the load. Thank you so much for shoveling the walk. Barid would do it, but he's never home early enough."

Emad's brows creased. "Are you sure that's all?"

"Well, we've had a fight and I think he's avoiding me." Jahana unplugged the squealing kettle. "I'm not sure we'll get through this one."

Emad wasn't sure he heard correctly, but he remained quiet, hoping she'd continue.

"But I don't want to talk about it right now. I appreciate your concern, but this is something I need to deal with."

Emad sat at the island, bobbing his tea bag up and down in his cup, watching the cranberry infuse the water. He was at a loss. Noosha always dealt with Jahana when she was upset. Did their fight have something to do with the secret her DNA test likely revealed?

"I'm sorry Jahni." And he was sorry. Sorry for the anguish a family secret caused her. Sorry he hadn't told her from the beginning about her past. Who would have thought she would find out by spitting in a tube?

Jahana stroked his hand and held his chin so he would look into her eyes. "You have nothing to be sorry about Baba. You raised me well. I'm grateful you were the male influence in my life."

In that moment he wanted to tell her everything. Cleanse his soul. But something in her eyes told him to wait. There was no doubt she knew something. But how much? Did she need to know everything? Maybe he could still shield her from some of it.

They sat in silence drinking tea. Emad's heart weighed heavy in his chest. "You know what your Maman would say?"

Jahana managed a smile in his direction.

"During difficult times she'd say the obstacles teach us to be better versions of ourselves and hardships help us appreciate happiness and…"

"You can't have one without the other." Jahana finished the sentence her maman would have said.

Emad chuckled. "You remember."

Silence fell over them again, lost in their own thoughts.

Watching Jahana struggle was almost as difficult as losing Noosha. He wanted to fix whatever weighed her down, but he had to wait for her to reach out and tell him what she needed. The parent role had shifted a long time ago. He had to let her make her own decisions. With the role change he learned more patience.

It wasn't his place to intrude on another man's marriage, but he wanted to grab Barid by the shoulders and shake respect for his daughter into him.

Another one of Noosha's wise sayings floated across his thoughts. *Life's complicated. We're all broken. Some of us more than others.*

****

Dinner came and went. Barid hadn't been home since Monday morning. The girls were used to him being away so didn't notice his extended absence. Jahana spent two nights hanging around the front door in case he decided to make an appearance. No more. She descended the stairs to the basement once the girls were in bed. She hadn't checked the MyGeneticFamily account since Friday night. Barid's bombshell inserted enough drama in her life, she didn't need to go looking for more. But curiosity got the better of her. Had her sister or mother responded to her queries?

When she opened the message board, there was a post from hlsi231, her mother. Jahana closed her eyes and took a few deep breaths, before sitting forward to read.

Dearest Jahana,

I'm sorry not to reach out before now. I wanted to with all my heart. But not sure you want to hear your story. It been so long since I hoped one day to find you. But it is how they say, double-edged sword? It also means you want to know story of your birth.

I am Jewish. I lived in Tehran with family till 1979 when Khomeini regime took power. My papa a businessman from Israel. We live in Tehran two years, but still had home in Jerusalem. The country in turmoil and very dangerous for Jews from Israel.

Days before we escaped, you born. I was fifteen and scared. My parents made me give you up for adoption. I considered abortion, but parents wouldn't allow and in the end I was glad. It's not that I never wanted you. I was young and afraid, that is all. I never had chance to hold you. They took you away to orphanage. The next week I returned to Israel with parents and brother.

The front door opened and Barid's footsteps echoed above. Jahana inhaled and climbed the stairs. He stood in the kitchen peering into the fridge. She stopped in the doorway, not knowing quite what to say. Barid turned, saw her and smiled, like nothing was different. Like he hadn't stayed away for two nights. Like he thought he could just decree a change in their marriage and she would go along with it. Jahana clenched her teeth, her face flushed. His smile dissolved.

"Now Jahana. I've given you time to see how helping Maha is what is important here. It's my duty to help her."

"Are you serious?" Jahana kept her voice low. "Do you really think this is magnanimous? That I could agree to another wife?"

She wanted to say mistress but knew that would set him off and result in an argument about the rights of Muslim men to provide for more than one wife. Wife is the only way he saw it.

"I've given you everything, Jahana. Asking for you to understand another woman's desperate situation and having the heart to help her out isn't asking too much."

"That's where the problem really lies. It seems you are getting more out of this than assisting a helpless woman. You get two beds, two families, a place to escape when one wife pisses you off."

Jahana would lose the argument if she lost her cool, and she was dangerously close to leaping over the edge.

"So, is that it? You want a second husband? So, you can escape me when I piss you off?"

Jahana swallowed to prevent herself from being dragged down and led in another direction, as only Barid could do. Twist around the facts and her own words to make this her fault. That wouldn't happen this time.

"If you want another wife, Barid, you'll have to grant me a divorce first. I'll not be part of a family where two women vie for your attention. And I'll not wait around for you to choose. Choose tonight. Is it me or Maha?"

Barid blinked and squinted his eyes, staring through her. She straightened. The line defining morality drawn.

"This is not over." He spun around and stomped toward the front door.

"Oh, yes, it is." Jahana stood resolute. Snow swirled in the open door just before it slammed with such force the windows rattled.

His headlights backed out of the driveway and turned down the street before her knees buckled, and she caught herself on the edge of the couch. She lowered herself to the cushions shaking. No tears pooled in her eyes or ran down her cheeks. She would not give him the satisfaction, whether or not he was there to see it.

Once the adrenaline abated, she rose, stood tall, and returned to the basement. Jiggling her mouse, the computer sprang to life and the message reopened.

> *I heard you were left in good hands at orphanage. Birth certificate to say Persian and make no mention of Jewish blood. You would be safe.*
>
> *But as a mother, even a 15-year-old mother, I worried. Would someone discover your Jewish heritage? I am grateful for no DNA testing in 1979.*
>
> *I rather not tell you about your father, but I suspect you would send questions until I do. It is not an easy story to tell. Please don't judge harshly, but I do not know your father's name. I have replayed the day you were conceived over and over in my mind, and I am convinced he was a Muslim man with status, although I don't know for sure. He was a good-looking man, someone of privilege, someone who got what he wanted.*
>
> *I walked home from school the day I met your father. Usually my papa would pick me up, but meetings delayed him and couldn't make it. I wasn't worried. It was a walk I done many times before the revolution. I was young, naïve and stupid. It seemed like he appeared out of nowhere.*

Suddenly he was walking beside me. I remember some militia slowing down and shouting at me asking if he was my brother. We weren't allowed to walk alone or with anyone other than our father or brother, so I replied yes, and they sped off. If I told the truth, I would likely be dead and you would never been born.

Your father seemed nice, telling me he would make sure I made it home, but there was something about him that gave me goosebumps. We walked past small lane when he pushed me into the alley. There is no easy way to say this. He raped me. There was nothing I could do. If I resisted, he would kill me. If I screamed and someone came, they would arrest me. I silently allowed him to do what he wanted to do. Lucky for me, it was over quick and I was close to home. I picked myself up and made it in my front door before another patrol. That was the last time I left our apartment until my parents took me to Israel. A doctor delivered you in my bedroom and took you away moments after I laid eyes on you.

It may not seem possible, but I loved you the moment you were born. I will never forgive that stranger for raping me, but I will be forever grateful I brought you into this world.

Jahana's bowels twisted.

CHAPTER EIGHTEEN

W hen the diarrhea stopped, dry heaves followed. Jahana leaned on the cool porcelain of the pedestal sink staring at her reflection in the mirror. Her face betrayed her soul.

Which are the rapist's parts? Is his evil embedded in my genes? Thank God I don't have sons.

Then it occurred to Jahana the Muslim part of her was the tainted part. The disgusting part. The only good bits were those created by the Jewish genes.

Ironic they raised me Muslim.

She turned on the cold water and splashed her face before wiping the toilet rim and flushing, pausing again in front of the mirror. *Why are my bowels so tied to my emotions?*

The creak of footsteps on the floor caused her heart to quicken. Was it Barid or the girls? Or an intruder? A shiver crept up her spine.

The bottom step to the basement creaked, and she slid the bathroom door closed. The click of the lock reverberating off the tiles. If it was one of the girls, she didn't want them to see her this way and if it was an intruder, she wanted a barrier between them. The steps approached and a solid knock landed on the door. The knock of an adult, not a child.

"Jahana, are you okay?"

Jahana exhaled and opened the door to face Barid. The shock of her appearance reflected in his expression.

"Not really."

His hand grasped her shoulder, and she recoiled.

"You'll be happy, I've made my decision and want to stay with you and the girls."

Jahana took a step back. "It's too late Barid. The minute you walked out the door you chose. I want a divorce."

The words hung in the silence between them. This was her choice; he would not make this decision for her.

"But I was just leaving to get some space. Give myself some time to think."

"There shouldn't have been a decision to make. Pack a few things and leave. You'll not be staying here tonight."

Jahana stepped forward and looked him in the eye.

His fists clenched and unclenched at his sides. Although her body trembled, she refused to look away, meeting his gaze until he turned.

"I'll give you some time to cool off. We can talk about this when you're in a better frame of mind."

Jahana ignored his comments, she'd been through enough tonight. Barid disappeared, his footsteps heavy on the floor above. The cold tiles soothed her when her strength dissolved and she crumpled to the floor. There were no more tears to cry. The front door slammed for the second time that night.

****

A spasm in her neck sent pain shooting down her spine and for a moment she wondered why she was on the bathroom floor, then it came rushing back.

In the kitchen the microwave blinked 5:00 am. The girls would be up in two hours. She opened the fridge and pulled out a cucumber, sliced off two pieces and carried them up to bed. Before climbing between the sheets, she set the alarm for 6:30, then turned off the lamp and lay on her back with the cucumbers covering her eyelids.

Back sleeping wasn't possible, so she didn't even try, letting her thoughts obsess. Did her parents know they'd raised a Jewish child? A product of rape? Jewish never appeared on the orphanage documents. Maybe her parents always thought they were raising a Persian Muslim child. But if so, why hide adoption from her?

Why hadn't she taken an Advil before laying down? Her heart pounded in her head. She removed the cucumber slices and shuffled to the bathroom, holding her head with both hands. Locating the Advil at the back of the drawer, she took out two and reached for the faucet. That's when she saw the note taped to the sink. *I love you.* It was Barid's meticulous handwriting.

She tore it into tiny pieces and deposited it in the garbage before swallowing the pills and returning to bed.

CHAPTER NINETEEN

The sun shimmered off the hardwood as Jahana sat on the edge of the bed, willing herself to move to the bathroom. She touched her eyes, still puffy, the cucumber a waste of time. She arched a stiff back and leaned from one side to the other, trying to work out the kinks from her nap on the bathroom floor. Easing herself off the bed, she dragged herself to the bathroom. In the shower she stood motionless while, the heat penetrated skin and warmed muscles.

All ready for work, she opened Sahba's door. The blankets lay on the floor in a heap, her knees tucked under her, arms under the pillow, face turned toward the wall. Jahana picked the blankets up and covered her, leaning down to kiss her head. "Time to get up sleepy head. It's Friday, you can sleep in tomorrow."

Sahba rolled onto her side, rubbing her eyes awake. Jahana understood why her parents didn't tell her the truth. How would she tell her girls? When was the right time? And she had to tell them about Barid too. It was tempting to preserve innocence for as long as possible.

Sahba touched her face and looked up. "Are you okay Maman?"

"Fine sweetheart. I'm just fine." She kissed her forehead and turned to the door. "If you're quick, you'll beat Cyra to the bathroom."

In front of Cyra's door, she paused, straightening and pasting on a smile before entering. How much had Cyra heard? She was a light sleeper. Did the door slamming or the yelling wake her?

"Time to rise and shine lazy bones. I think Sahba's already in the bathroom."

Cyra lay in bed awake and glared at Jahana, eyes softening when she looked at Jahana's face. "I'm up Maman." She threw back the covers and sat up, swinging her feet over the side.

Jahana kissed the top of her head. "It's going to be okay; I promise." Cyra nodded but didn't ask.

Before starting the car, she messaged Mishal.

Need to talk. Can you meet me for an early lunch?

Mishal responded immediately.

Yes, see you at 11:30.

Perfect.

****

Jahana read Mishal her mother's email. When she looked up from her phone, Mishal opened her mouth to speak, but before she responded, Jahana raised her hand. "That's not all. Barid and I separated last night."

Jahana watched Mishal blink and swallow, open her mouth to say something, then pause. She reached across the table and clasped her hand.

"Oh Jahana. Are you separated because of the results?" Mishal released her hand and picked up a napkin to pat her eyes.

"No. No, I haven't told him anything about the results. This is my decision not his."

"But last time we talked I was left with the impression you wouldn't leave him. What changed your mind?"

It was Jahana's turn to wipe her eyes. "I asked him to choose between us and he left to think about it. When he returned I told him it was too late. If he had to think about it, I didn't want to be with him. I asked him to leave." Jahana let go of Mishal's hand and sat back in her chair deflated.

"And he did?" Mishal lowered her chin and looked over her glasses.

"Yes, for one night at least. I suspect he'll return and try to patch things up. But my mind is made up," Jahana bounced a clenched fist on the table.

"I'm proud of you. You're a strong woman."

"I can't believe all of this came crashing in at once. If Barid finds out about my past, there's no telling what he'll do."

"He gave up his rights to an opinion when he took on a mistress. Will you tell him about your results? And what about your baba? Are you going to tell him?"

"I'll have to think about telling Barid. There could be all kinds of hell to deal with if he knows. As for Baba, I'll tell him eventually. In my heart I'm sure he knows some of the story, I'm just not sure how much."

Mishal nodded but remained silent.

"I'm sorry to have to tell you before you go help at the boys' school this afternoon, but I needed to talk to someone. Are you okay?"

"Oh, don't worry about me. I'm here to support you." Mishal leaned forward. "You're the same person you've always been. How you were conceived and who your birth parents are don't make a smidgeon of difference. If it changes your relationship with anyone, they shouldn't have been part of your life to begin with."

Jahana needed those words. She watched Mishal walk out of the cafeteria. Somehow sharing her sorrow helped ease the burden.

That evening while Jahana made dinner she flinched every time the girls walked into the kitchen. She expected Barid to show up for dinner, knowing she wouldn't say anything in front of the girls. And she wouldn't have said anything. But despite the many skips of her heart, he never showed.

Once the girls were in bed, she checked the front door lock and retreated to the basement. The tang of vomit lingered in the stale air. She found a can of Febreze in the bathroom cupboard and sprayed. With a fresh linen scent covering the trauma of the night before, she settled in to write a carefully crafted email.

Dear…

I'm not sure how to address this email, 'Dear hlsi231'? 'Dear Maman'? I'm not comfortable calling you either of those things. You are more than hlsi231 and yet you don't fill the maman role because someone else filled that role my entire life. So, I'll leave it unaddressed and let you fill in the blank.

There are so many reasons for me to thank you, but my heart is hurting, and it's hard to be thankful knowing I'm a product of a sexual assault. I can't imagine how hard it was for you to write that message, let alone acknowledge that I exist, so that's where I'll start.

Thank you for giving me an existence and for loving me even though I represented so much evil and hardship. Having me and then letting me go to be raised by wonderful people was a selfless act. One I can never thank you enough for.

Someday I hope to tell you about my life, but today I'm too exhausted. But I want you to know my life has been good and I'm blessed with two beautiful daughters. I'm glad you had a second daughter too.

I want to apologize for the man who raped you, but no apology from me would ever be enough. Maybe one day we can talk about that in person.

Thank you again for reaching out to me even though it was painful for both of us.

Jahana stared at the blinking cursor, finger resting on the mouse. She pressed down and sent the message.

CHAPTER TWENTY

A few weeks passed without visiting her baba. Jahana took a deep breath and stepped out onto the plowed street and secured a toehold in the ridge of snow between her and the sidewalk, teetering her way to the top before sinking to her knee. The shoveled driveway looked like the preferred option but she was committed now. Her leg swung over and pulled her limb from its frosty hold. On the sidewalk she stomped her way to the step and rang the doorbell.

Her baba answered the door, looking past Jahana. "Where are the girls?"

Jahana stepped into the house and closed the door. "Well, glad to see you too." She smiled and kissed each of his cheeks. "I dropped them off at friends' houses. First day of Christmas break and they've got sleepovers already."

"How wonderful to have you all to myself. Come, I'll make you some tea."

Jahana followed him into the kitchen hoping to start a conversation she'd rather avoid.

"Baba, you know that DNA testing I did?"

Emad's back faced her as he reached into the cupboard for tea, his arm halted in mid-air before setting the cannister on the counter.

"Well, I've been following up on matches. What do you know about my adoption?"

Emad wheeled around, eyes red and glassy, face flushed. He held up his hand, waving it towards Jahana.

"Stop. No, we're not talking about this."

Jahana had never seen him like this. She backed up as he moved towards her.

"Please leave."

He waved toward the front door. Jahana stumbled to pull on her boots and grab her coat, not bothering to put it on before stepping out of the house. Tears slid down her cheeks as she climbed into the driver's seat. The snow on her boots told her she'd climbed through the snow bank again, but she didn't recall.

What had she done? Why hadn't she eased into it? Of course, it was a shock.

The front door remained closed, she sat in her car. His frame of mind frightened her, but what could she do? He'd just kicked her out of the house. She called, but he wouldn't answer. A movement in the living room window caught her eye, he was waiting for her to leave. She'd give him space to digest the fact she knew about her adoption and call him later.

When she arrived home, Barid's car filled the driveway blocking access to the garage. She parked on the street and stood on the step, taking a deep breath before opening the door. Tension filled the air, but she took her time, hanging up her coat and setting her purse on the closet shelf. The hairs on the back of her neck bristled. *I need to get the locks changed.* She walked past the living room and stopped. A cold, stony face watched her from the couch.

"Where're the girls?" Barid's voice held the edge of someone about to explode.

"At sleepovers." As soon as the words escaped, she realized she'd left the whole evening open. "Oh, and Baba's coming over for dinner." It sounded like the lie it was.

Barid's face softened, and he cleared his throat. "Jahana, I want to apologize. I'm only trying to help Maha out of a difficult situation. And yes, we've become close, but I want to work things out with you."

She paused, choosing words carefully. "Barid you've lost my trust. I don't want to work on this marriage. It's over."

He rose from the couch stepping towards her one hand waving in her face, the other clenched by his side. His breath and small prickles of spittle landed on her face.

"You're an idiot! I'll make life so miserable; you'll wish you'd never met me."

Jahana closed her eyes, and exhaled, shielding herself from his barrage of threats. The next words, however, opened her eyes and caused her bowels to twist.

"I'll sue for custody of the girls. Not shared custody. Full custody."

Jahana's heart quickened. She stepped back, he followed.

"What do you know about looking after the girls?" Her eyes darted, looking for a way around him. A smile cut through his anger and she realized, Maha would be the one looking after them.

The wall unforgiving behind her, Barid's sneer inches away. She lifted her head, meeting his eyes, and growled. "Get out."

He backed away and paced, a scowl replacing his smile, eyes fixed on her. "You'll regret this."

Stomping to the door, he grabbed his coat. "You've brought this on yourself." The door slammed behind him.

Jahana returned to the living room and watched him pull out onto the street, snow spewing from his tires as he accelerated out of sight. Frantically rifling through pockets, she searched for her phone before realizing it was in her purse. The first locksmith that appeared on a Google search received her business.

Just as she hung up, a text appeared from her baba, he was on his way over.

****

"Have I lost you too?" Emad looked like a little boy standing on her doorstep.

"Oh Baba, you'll never lose me." Jahana stepped outside and pulled him into a hug. "Take off your jacket and let me make some tea."

"I'm just going to use the washroom first." Emad choked back tears.

He needed to pull himself together. Jahana didn't need to see his tears. He dabbed at his eyes in the bathroom mirror and took a deep breath. *She's not angry with me.* Their conversation needed to be truthful. The secret formed a dark cave deep inside him for so long. An ulcer. But he never knew how to right the wrong or whether he should. Today they would expose the truth. As frightened as he was, he was also relieved.

Jahana stood in the kitchen pouring tea into his favourite cups. She motioned for him to sit beside her at the island.

"You are my baba. The place you hold in my heart will always be there. It doesn't matter that we don't carry the same genes, you are the man who raised me, the man who holds my heart."

Emad lowered his head and cleared his throat. "Thank you for saying that, but I fear once you know the entire truth you won't feel the same." He blew on the tea sending swirls of steam into the air.

Jahana shifted in her seat. "I'll love you even more. Please, leave nothing out."

There was a long pause before Emad began.

"Some of what I've told you over the years is true. Noosha lost two baby boys. One a year before you were born and the second the same day you were born. He wasn't your twin, but we always thought of him that way. I remember standing outside the nursery admiring the babies, wishing one was my baby boy. Their pink little faces peered out of swaddled blankets in the bassinets. I recognized a man off to the side watching a nurse place a baby in an incubator." Emad stared at the counter top, scratching something off its surface then looking up at Jahana with a wistful smile. "You were yellow."

Emad sipped his tea before continuing. "The man's name was Afsar. He ran the local orphanage, and we'd met him at charity events over the years. He was a kind man and when his eyes met mine that day, he approached me. Noosha was resting, and I was trying to delay telling anyone about our dead baby."

Tears pooled in Emad's eyes and Jahana brought the tissue box from on top of the fridge. He took a tissue and bowed his head before continuing.

"Afsar held my hand as I told him about our loss, he was a great comfort." Emad paused and raised his eyes to Jahana before continuing. "Then he told me about you. He took me into a side room to talk and he told me about his worries. Told me your story." Emad's voice cracked. "Are you sure you want me to keep going?"

"Yes Baba."

"Afsar told me you were born to a Jewish mother." Emad paused. Jahana nodded.

"And…" Tears pooled in his eyes and he choked on a sob escaping his throat.

"It's okay Baba."

"And she was raped. That's how she became pregnant."

Emad almost whispered the last words, resting his head in his hands. Jahana rubbed his knee.

"It's okay Baba."

Emad looked up. "You knew? How? When did you find out?"

Emad took Jahana's hand between both of his.

"My birth mother messaged me through the DNA site a few days ago and she told me her story. But please go on, I want to hear it from your perspective."

The doorbell rang, startling them both.

"Are you expecting someone?"

For a second Jahana looked confused and then recollection spread across her face.

"Oh, ah yes, it's the locksmith. I'll tell you about why later. Please just give me a minute and I'll be right back."

Emad heard Jahana telling the locksmith to change the front and back door locks. She asked for number pad combination locks. *That would make sense for the girls, easier to remember a code than carry a key they always misplaced.* The cool winter air reached him from the open door and he wrapped his fingers around his cup. *Why would Jahana pick a day like today to have the locks changed?*

Jahana returned to the kitchen sliding the pocket door to keep out the cold air and give them some privacy.

"Please go on Baba."

Emad sipped his tea and continued. "Afaar told me he feared for your safety. The regime worried him. And he feared if anyone found out about your Jewish blood, you'd never be adopted. Afsar was a kind man and would never refuse a child, but he was at a loss as to what would be best for you. None of your paperwork was completed yet, partly because he was trying to decide what to put on the forms and partly because he was busy getting you medical care." Emad took another sip of tea.

"As Afsar talked, a plan formed. You were undocumented, and we hadn't told anyone about losing a baby. I took Afsar to Noosha, and we discussed adoption. If we proceeded, we couldn't tell anyone. Noosha's family was already on the Khomeini radar, and we didn't want to draw any additional attention." Emad felt the weight of the lies lifting as he spoke.

"In those days, it was easy to complete the paperwork without oversight. The hospital didn't check on it, so we decided to make you a twin to our beloved baby boy. When the nurse handed you to Noosha, you found your home in her arms."

Emad looked up into Jahana's eyes and saw her tears.

"Thank you, Baba, thank you." Jahana blew her nose and wiped at the tears streaming down her cheeks.

"I'm sorry we never told you. At first, we feared for your safety. We didn't want someone figuring out your story, so immigrating to Canada after your birth also worked out. We had a fresh start, all of us."

"I understand Baba."

"I'm sorry you had to find out. You could have lived your whole life not knowing any of this pain. But I'm glad your mother has found you. I can't imagine what she's gone through all these years."

They sat in silence, lost in their own thoughts. Emad looked up. "Have you told Barid?"

Jahana wiped her eyes and cleared her throat.

"Barid. No Baba, I haven't. I'll tell him at some point, but we're going through some things right now and I don't want to bring it up." Jahana paused, her eyes shifting from him to the floor. Then she cleared her throat and continued. "He's decided he wants a second wife."

Emad's eyes widened and he jumped to his feet, fists clenching and unclenching. Jahana squeezed his arm. "It's okay Baba, I've already told him I won't agree. Told him to choose, but he took too long to decide and I asked for a divorce. When I got home from your place today, he was in the living room. He left furious just before you messaged. That's the reason for the locksmith."

"Why would he think you'd agree to this?"

"Because he's threatening to take the girls away if I don't. He wants full custody." Jahana's voice cracked and her hands shook, but she continued. "It's all bluster, he's never looked after the girls. They'd just be a burden to him. To tell you the truth, I'm not sure if telling him I'm Jewish would make things better or worse. On the one hand, he may not want custody of the girls because of their Jewish genes, which is the scenario I'm leaning towards. But if he's bent on punishing me, using my Jewish genes against me in court, might be a strategy. An argument to discredit my ability to raise the girls in a Muslim home."

"No court would consider that."

The sliding door opened, and the locksmith entered to pass through to the back door. He glanced from them to the pile of tissues and continued to the back door.

"I'd like to stay over tonight. Would that be okay?"

"Oh Baba, that would be great. Thank you."

CHAPTER TWENTY-ONE

"**H**ow can a heart be both full and empty of love?" Her baba sat on the couch, the girls on either side.

They had been talking about the book, The Conference of Birds, and her baba asked if he could read it with them. The girls were much more excited about reading the book when he was there. So Jahana gave him the place of honor between the girls and she sat across the room in the chair, listening in.

"Good question Cyra. Do you ever love someone, but are angry at them too?"

Cyra nodded, glancing quickly at Jahana.

"So, your heart is both full and empty of love at the same time, don't you think?"

"I guess so." Cyra tucked her feet up under her on the couch.

"And when you're angry with someone you love, isn't it worse than being angry at someone you don't really know?"

Again, Cyra nodded.

"So, like the book says in the Valley of Astonishment and Bewilderment you are prey to sadness and dejection. How many times do we complain about things that ultimately make us happy? We might say we don't want to go home at the end of a vacation, but really shouldn't we say we get to go home? There are many people in this world without a home and yet we complain about ours. We are astonished and bewildered at the same time."

Sahba stared at her babayi, a smile playing at the corners of her mouth. "You are so smart, Babayi."

Jahana smiled. It was as if they forgot she was sitting there. It warmed her heart to see the girls bonding with her baba. His words had an effect on her too. Here she was wishing for Noosha, yet she found another mother, still alive, still able to talk to her. How lucky was she?

Her guilt over searching out her mother dissipated. One mother would not replace the other, she was lucky to have two.

And yet, she did not want to find her biological father. The despicable acts he performed in his life could not be forgiven. He did not deserve to know her.

Jahana couldn't stop thinking this was a test. Would she make it out of the Valley of Astonishment and Bewilderment? Or would she remain there, stuck by her anger and inability to forgive?

Lost in her own thoughts, she watched the girls wrestle with her baba, clearly, they had given up on the book for tonight.

CHAPTER TWENTY-TWO

“**B**arid called. He says he met with a lawyer to discuss fighting for sole custody of the girls.” Jahana’s voice was breathless, panicked.

“Wait, what?” Mishal whispered into the phone, hoping not to disturb Hamid as she scrambled out of bed ducking into the ensuite and closing the door.

“Mishal so sorry, were you sleeping?”

“No, no, I was in bed checking Facebook on my phone. It’s okay, I’m in the bathroom with the door closed now. Okay, take a deep breath and tell me what's going on."

"Barid just called to tell me he's suing for full custody. As much as I hoped he'd calm down and give up on this, he's holding it over me. Trying to force me to agree to a dual marriage. If I agree to his terms of marriage, the girls can stay at the house and he'll live with us one week a month. But I can't do it, Mishal, I just can't!"

Mishal paced the floor between the tub and vanity. "Okay. No judge will give him custody over you. Let him try."

"But 50/50 custody is a real possibility, and that's too much. I don't want the girls having to stay with him. He hasn't called them since he moved out and is just using them as pawns to get what he wants."

"You can argue he's coercing you into a polygamous marriage. That won't win him points in court."

"True. But it's his word against mine. He'll deny it."

Jahana was right. He wouldn't quit until he had everything. There was no one to corroborate her story.

"There's something that might deter him."

Mishal stopped pacing. "No. I can guess what you're thinking. That's not a good idea, it could backfire so easily."

Jahana's breathing slowed, words spilled out in measured sentences. "If he knows about our Jewish ancestry, he'll move on. He won't want anyone knowing the girls have Jewish blood, his Palestinian roots have jaded his views of all Jews. If I tell him about my ancestry and threaten to bring it up in court, that might be the end of it."

"Or give him more ammunition. He could use it against you claiming you won't bring the girls up in the Muslim faith? Maybe he won't care about exposing your ancestry." Mishal's eyes widened. "Or maybe he'll take them to Palestine and never come back?"

Jahana shivered. "I've thought of that too. It concerns me more than the possibility of a judge siding with him in concerns over the girls being raised Muslim. I have no problem signing a document promising to continue my Islam faith. Putting everything out there is my biggest hope."

"I'm just afraid he'll get mad enough to hurt you. Husbands murder wives over less. Promise someone will be with you when you tell him."

"Oh, Barid would never harm me or the girls, but don't worry, I won't meet with him alone."

****

The cold rush of air crept under her hijab when the coffee shop door opened and Barid sauntered in, stopping to study the menu board. His gaze never wandered over the tables; his needs came first.

Once he ordered and waited for his double latte, it was always a double latte, he glanced around the room. When he saw Emad his eyes widened, but he glanced away, fingers tapping the counter.

Jahana asked for the meeting, letting him think she wanted to talk about their relationship, giving him hope she reconsidered his proposal. But now with her baba, he'd know there was more to the meeting than she'd let on.

Barid retrieved the coffee he ordered and turned to face her; a wide smile pasted on his face. Emad rose and Barid shook his hand.

"So nice to see you Emad. You're looking well."

Jahana couldn't stand watching Barid try to charm her father, pretend to be the man he wasn't.

Jahana took a deep breath. "This meeting isn't about our relationship."

Barid's smile faded, the twinkle in his eye flattened. He took a sip of his coffee before pushing back and crossing his legs.

Jahana continued. "I've followed up on that DNA test kit you gave me for our anniversary last year. Turns out there are a few surprises that took me a while to sort through."

Barid uncrossed his legs and leaned forward, a smile returning to his face. "Those distant cousins pan out?"

Jahana licked her lips. "Not exactly. I had some ancestry surprises that caused me to question whether my parents were my biological parents, so Mishal got tested."

Barid looked from Jahana to Emad and back again before resting his arms on the table.

She'd practiced this, but couldn't remember how to ease into it. "Turns out Mishal isn't my cousin and Baba isn't my biological father."

Barid looked to Emad for confirmation. Emad nodded.

"You knew this and let me marry her?"

Jahana placed a hand on her father's arm. He agreed to stay silent no matter what Barid said.

"Oh, it's much worse than that, Barid. Not only isn't Baba my blood, neither was Maman. I'm adopted."

"So, you're not a princess after all?" He leaned back in his chair, clasping his hands behind his head. "And you had our children not knowing who you were?"

"Now wait a minute, Jahni knew nothing about this." Emad glanced at Jahana and sat back in his chair.

Barid leaned forward, pointing at Emad. "But you did. You let me marry her thinking she was your child? Why would you keep this a secret, unless of course you were ashamed of adopting her? What kind of father are you?" Barid sneered. "Oh yeah, you're not a father." A forced laugh, escaped his lips.

Jahana leaned forward trying to shield her baba from Barid's onslaught. "Okay Barid, hear me out. There's more to this, and it doesn't get any better. My birth mother was only fifteen when I was born and she left me in the care of an orphanage in Tehran. She fled Tehran shortly after because she was…" Jahana paused.

Barid threw his hands in the air. "Because she was what? An Alien?" He chuckled again, but his eyes darted from Jahana to Emad.

"No Barid, because she was Jewish."

Jahana decided before the meeting not to tell him she was a product of rape. She waited for a reaction. But he sat quietly, like the words hadn't registered, before bursting into laughter. Loud belly laughs that caught the attention of other patrons, who looked on smiling.

"Nice try." He leaned in closer and hissed. "I'd know if I married a Jew. This is a trick to get me to back away from the child custody suit. Right? You're smarter than I give you credit for." He leaned back in his chair again. A pleasant smile pasted on his face. The other customers returned to their conversations.

Heat traveled up Jahana's neck and into her cheeks. *What did I ever see in you?*

"I'm not making this up Barid, I'd never make up a story like this."

Barid snorted and rose, leaning over Jahana, his voice low. "I wasn't born yesterday, Jahana. Good try though. See you in court."

He turned towards the door and stepped outside without looking back.

Emad placed a hand on Jahana's shoulder. "Whether Barid believes you or not, you've planted the seed."

Jahana's fists clenched and unclenched under the table. "I'll have to prove it. But how will I get him to look at the results? He'll never admit he married a Jew and has two Jewish children. Not without proof."

"Are you sure he'll give up, or will it spur him on to take the girls from you?" Emad's face was ashen.

"I can't imagine him wanting the world to know he married a Jewish woman. My gut tells me he'll give up, but with Barid it's hard to tell."

Emad sat in silence. Barid's departure hung in the air between them. "Will you have to show Barid the results or will the threat of bringing it up in court be enough?"

"Barid's always been a risk taker. If he thinks this is all made up, he might just pursue child custody harder. Anger has always motivated his actions." Jahana took a sip of coffee and grimaced.

"But if you play all your cards, it may work against you. If a judge sympathizes with the religious component and worries about children being raised with the Hebrew Bible rather than the Quran, it might work against you. There's no way a judge would give him sole custody for that, but it might assure Barid a 50:50 split. And you don't want that either."

"But he'll get 50:50 custody even if I don't bring up being Jewish. And it's his word against mine regarding the second wife. I need to show the DNA evidence before we get anywhere near a trial."

"If your mother's message gets brought into court, he'll find out about the rape. Do you want that brought up at a trial?"

"Oh Baba, right now I don't know what I want, other than for Barid to leave us alone. I'll have to think on this. Hopefully, time provides a solution." Jahana slipped on her coat.

"Promise you'll talk to me before doing anything." Emad buttoned up his jacket.

"So, you can talk me out of it?"

Emad stopped what he was doing, then saw a smile spread across her face. "But seriously Jahni, you need to file for divorce soon. What you told him today will make a bigger impact if he sees you're serious."

"Perhaps Baba, acting quickly might be important. He thinks I'm trapped and hopes I'll take him back." Jahana pulled on a toque and took her gloves out of her pocket.

Emad sighed. "I'm so sorry this secret put you in this situation. If you'd known before you married, you wouldn't be in this mess."

Jahana leaned on the table. "Baba, Mishal pointed out if I hadn't married Barid I wouldn't have Cyra and Sahba in my life." She picked up her gloves, slid her hands into them, and pulled them tight.

"I hadn't thought of it that way." Emad realized he had focused on the fallout from the secret, not the possibility of life without his granddaughters.

"Are you okay if I tell your uncle before he hears about it from Mishal?"

"Let me tell Sahba and Cyra first. I'm not sure when I'll do it, but I'll let you know when I do."

"I can be there when you tell them."

"No, this is something I need to do myself. I hope they'll talk to you about it after though."

Emad patted Jahana's shoulder before they left the coffee shop. "I hope we find a new normal soon."

CHAPTER TWENTY-THREE

S ahba's eyes widened. "So, that's how the book ends? Saying there is no God?"

"I think it's saying we are all God." Cyra sat up peering over Jahana at Sahba.

"I agree Cyra. I think the poem suggests God works through all of us. God isn't one being, but is every living thing."

Silence fell over the bedroom.

Sahba turned to Jahana and whispered. "But when we die, we all become one?"

"I think that's what this poem is saying. When we die, we are no longer separate, we mix together like drops in the ocean."

"Cool." Cyra's eyes brightened.

"I don't think it's cool at all. It means that Mamani isn't watching over us. She's gone forever." A sob escaped Sahba and a hiccup followed.

Jahana maneuvered her arm under her and pulled her close. "That's not how I see it. I see it as Mamani has everyone who has ever died watching over us. She became part of the big energy force and that energy becomes part of us."

Sahba wiggled away from Jahana and lay quietly staring up at the ceiling, one tear sliding to the pillow.

Jahana continued. "I agree with Cyra, I think it's cool too. And I like the statement at the end that talks about how everyone is born with possibilities to become whoever they want. I think we need to be aware of being influenced by others to believe what they think. We need to resist becoming what they want us to be and instead think for ourselves. We should let that energy force influence and guide us to make the right decisions for ourselves. It's important to remember to question and think beyond what people say to form our own thoughts and beliefs."

"So being stubborn is a good thing." Sahba's face lit up.

Jahana chuckled. "Yes, being stubborn is a good thing if it's because you're exploring what you think and not resisting other's ideas just because you want to be contrary for no good reason. But yes, it's always good to question."

****

"I'm just getting groceries, but want to stop by on my way home if that's okay?" Mishal tucked the phone between her shoulder and neck as she pushed the shopping cart through the snow to her car.

She worried about Jahana; they hadn't talked for a week. While she vowed to give her space to figure things out, she couldn't wait any longer. It was Saturday afternoon during Christmas break and the boys were at home playing video games with Hamid.

"I'd love to see you."

Mishal couldn't remember the last time she'd been to Jahana's house. As long as Barid was around, she never felt comfortable stopping by. As she pulled in front and parked a pang of nostalgia hit her. Growing up, this house had been a second home to her. It always brought back warm feelings.

"Baba took the girls to a movie," Jahana explained as Mishal closed the door and stomped the snow off her boots.

"Oh, it smells good in here. Looks like I might have stopped by at just the right time." Mishal sat down as Jahana poured tea. The fresh made biscuits along with cream and jam sat on the table between them with plates and cutlery.

"It's so nice to be back in this house."

Jahana never discussed Mishal's lack of visits. They both knew the reason she didn't stop by.

"You should sit in my kitchen more often, you belong here." Jahana smiled and seemed more at peace than she had in years.

"How are you? How are things with Barid?" Mishal reached for a biscuit, cut it and placed a dollop of thick clotted cream and strawberry jam on each half. Her mouth watered in anticipation.

"I'm surprisingly well, but things with Barid are strained. Baba and I met him at a coffee-shop last Saturday and I told him about being Jewish and adopted."

Mishal set her biscuit down and leaned forward. "And how did that go?"

Tears pooled in Jahana's eyes. "He laughed in my face. Said I'm making it all up to stop him from filing for custody. Basically, he thinks I'm lying." Jahana wiped her eyes, then reached for a biscuit.

"Are you kidding? So now what?"

"Show him the results and threaten to bring them out in court. I'll also file for divorce this coming week. He needs to understand I'm serious about moving ahead and won't be intimidated by a custody threat."

"Won't the threat of this coming out in court be enough to keep him from pursuing custody? Do you really have to prove it?" Mishal hated the idea of backing Barid into a corner. Who knows what he might do? She picked up a biscuit and bit into it, the sweet rich flavour of the jam and cream mixing with the savoury pastry exploded in her mouth.

"I'm not sure he'll take it seriously unless he has proof. I'm sure once he believes me, he won't want anyone to know his wife and children are Jewish and that will be his downfall. Palestinian roots will probably stop him from pursuing anything, which is what I'm banking on." Jahana sipped her tea, worry buried in the crease on her forehead.

"Baba also thinks a threat is enough. But Barid's a gambler. He's gambling on me lying. He needs proof."

"I'm afraid for your safety. Is he capable of hurting you or the girls?"

"Baba's worried too. But Barid's all bluster. His ego's his undoing. He wouldn't want to sully his reputation over me."

"Maybe, but please tread carefully." The biscuit sat heavy in the pit of Mishal's stomach. She took a long swallow of tea.

"Trust me, I'm giving it lots of thought. First, I'll tell the girls tonight and listen to their concerns before I decide about which way to go with this."

"That's a big step. This has to be so difficult." Mishal leaned forward; her expression intense. "Please make sure you don't meet with Barid alone. I'll be there if you want me to."

"Thanks, Mishal, I'll let you know."

CHAPTER TWENTY-FOUR

"**G**irls you've probably been wondering about your baba." Jahana took a breath, not knowing quite how to start the conversation. "I told you Baba, and I are separated, but I plan to ask him for a divorce this week." The words came out harsher than Jahana planned. Cyra's eyes pooled. Sahba set her taco down.

"This is difficult to understand and I'm sorry. But I want you to know what's happening." There was a long pause. Jahana let her words sink in.

"Where will we live?" Sahba looked up, her brows knit in concern.

"I want you to live with me, but your baba wants you to live with him." Cyra and Sahba looked at each other than back at Jahana.

"I want to live with you." Cyra's voice was desperate and Sahba nodded her head in agreement.

Jahana rested her hands on the table. "What if you spent part of your time with me and part with your baba?" She held her breath, afraid of their response.

"I want to see Baba." Cyra paused, struggling to find words to continue. "But live with you. Baba's never home."

Jahana exhaled. "Is that what you want too Sahba?"

Sahba nodded. "Baba doesn't look after us."

Jahana let out a slow breath. They were in agreement.

"That's how I'd like it too."

Jahana noticed they both brightened, but what they didn't understand was they might not get their wish.

"There's something else. Remember how Baba bought that DNA kit for me last year for our anniversary?"

The girls nodded.

"Well I've followed up on the results and learned I'm half Jewish."

"Oh, Baba wouldn't like that. Is that why you're getting divorced?" Cyra's eyes widened.

"No, no the divorce has nothing to do with the DNA test. I've told Baba, but I haven't shown him the printed results yet. I investigated further and also learned I'm adopted. Your babayi and mamani adopted me from an orphanage just before they immigrated to Canada. My biological maman is from Israel and my baba is from Iran. My maman was only two years older than you are Cyra when she had me."

Cyra's jaw dropped.

"She couldn't take care of me, so her parents arranged for me to go to an orphanage. Mamani and Babayi were so kind to take me in. Because the government in Iran was executing Jewish people at that time, they pretended I was their baby."

"What about your real baba?"

Jahana hoped not to tell them about her biological father tonight, but Sahba was always the thinker, the one who could cut through the clutter and find that all important question others may overlook. Jahana thought of glossing over his story, but decided there had been too many secrets and the girls were old enough to know.

"He wasn't a very nice man. He hurt my mother, and she never saw him again."

"Oh Maman, I'm so sorry." Cyra understood.

"It's okay, sweetheart, I'm glad I grew up in Canada with Maman and Baba. They will always be my parents."

Sahba and Cyra climbed off their chairs and wrapped their arms around her. Jahana's eye's filled with tears. In that moment she knew her journey was taking her where it needed to go.

****

Jahana waited for Mishal and Emad, settling into a small table in the back of the coffee shop, away from the noise and ears of most of the patrons. Talking with Sahba and Cyra cemented her resolve, and she promised to tell them her plan once she'd decided.

Mishal arrived first, Emad shortly after. They ordered beverages and settled in beside Jahana.

"I've talked to Cyra and Sahba and decided how to approach Barid."

Mishal sipped her tea; Emad stirred his coffee.

"I need to show Barid the results so he knows I'm not bluffing."

Mishal lowered her coffee cup.

Emad laid his spoon on the table. "Are you sure?"

"Positive, it's the best chance to deter Barid from seeking any kind of custody. Shared custody is too likely. My only hope that he'll walk away from the girls is to make him believe me. The girls don't want to live with him. This is the only way to stop him from pursuing custody."

Emad grasped Jahana's hand. "What if he hurts you or the girls? I'm worried this will push him over the edge."

"Baba if I don't provide evidence, he'll think I'm bluffing. Whether I present it now or in court, he'll know the truth. Why wait until court?"

Emad threw his hands in the air. "Consider the risk."

Jahana placed both hands on the table and leaned forward. "I'm done with the lies and pretending. This is something I have to do. The girls want to live with me full time and visit Barid occasionally. The only chance that scenario will play out is to produce the evidence. If he still takes me to court, so be it, I won't be any worse off."

"But what if he gets violent? You didn't know him when you married him, what if you still don't? Who knows what he'll do if he feels trapped?" Emad's eyes pleaded with her.

"I'm banking on his ego. He wouldn't want to draw attention that might tarnish his reputation. It would almost be as bad as people finding out he married a Jew. I've thought this through from every angle and am convinced I have to tell him."

Emad ran a hand through his hair and leaned back.

Mishal looked from Jahana to Emad and back again. "I agree it's the only solution that may allow full custody of the girls. And I also understand your concern Uncle Emad, but I trust Jahana knows how Barid will react better than either of us."

Emad shook his head, slipped on his jacket and walked out without another word. Jahana looked to Mishal for guidance.

"Don't worry, he'll come around."

Jahana buried her head in her hands. "Why can't Baba trust me?"

"Listen, he loves you and those girls more than anything and he's afraid that's all. Give him time."

Jahana's breathing slowed. Mishal was the voice of reason. Her baba had to stand by and watch her take a chance he had never taken.

"Just promise to bring me along when you talk to Barid?"

"Promise." It was what Mishal needed to hear, but Jahana wasn't convinced having Mishal present was the best idea.

****

A whisper of air fell across Jahana when she closed her front door and crumpled to the floor, sobbing. At the coffee shop in front of Mishal and her baba she'd been strong, but her world lay before her in shambles. Jahana hadn't seen the destruction coming despite the warnings from Mishal to be careful and her baba's anger over taking the test. She'd ignored their advice.

Now her baba told her to think about what she was doing and begged her to change her mind. And again, she ignored him. The what ifs paralyzed her, the way they must have paralyzed her parents. But they allowed that paralysis to prevent them from telling her the truth. If she hadn't taken that DNA test, their secret would have died with them.

She vowed to learn from her parents' mistakes. She understood why they initially kept the secret, but why didn't they tell her when she was older? Would she look back one day and see the errors of her own logic in telling Barid about the lie? Without the benefit of hindsight, it looked like the right thing to do.

Jahana closed her eyes and continued to lean against the door, hugging her knees to her chest. The cold from the door seeped into her spine, but she remained seated on the floor, deep in thought. There were scenarios to consider, but she knew the first one wasn't an option. Sahba would be eighteen in seven years. She couldn't share Barid with another woman for seven years. Besides, now that the girls knew their ancestry, was it even an option? She couldn't ask them to keep their ancestry a secret. Once Barid was convinced she wasn't lying about the Jewish ancestry, he might decide she could have the girls full time or he might decide to take the girls from her so he could control her and the girls' futures.

She released her knees and kicked off her boots. *Am I being selfish wanting the girls to myself?*

Jahana sighed and crawled to her feet, hanging her jacket in the closet. In the doorway to the kitchen her knees buckled, and she grabbed the door jamb for support. On the island sat a bouquet of red roses, and a card with her name scrawled in Barid's handwriting. *He's been here. Maybe he still is.* Acid rose in the back of her throat. Her knees weakened. She forced herself to straighten, walking into the living room first. No Barid. Was *Baba right to worry about my safety?*

Knowing she'd be unable to rest until she searched the entire house, she stumbled to the top of the basement stairs and flicked on the light. He wouldn't sit in the dark waiting for me, but he might be in the office searching for DNA results. She took a deep breath and descended the stairs, hesitating before reaching out to flick on the light in her office. Everything appeared as she left it. She continued the search, clearing the basement before returning to the main floor. Back at the front door she looked up to the landing, their bedroom. Was he perched on the bed, waiting, smiling as he heard her scour the house for him? Anger rose, bowels clenched. She marched up the stairs and flung open the bedroom door. Nothing. A quick search of the walk-in closet and the en-suite turned up no sign of him. She continued her search of the girls' bedrooms, Sahba's last. *He's not here.* A sigh escaped into the quiet and she lowered herself onto the bed.

How had he gotten in? Guessed the code? She'd made it easy for the girls to remember, their birthdays, she'd have to change it. Her baba's fears had overcome her. Barid never physically hurt her or the kids and she felt confident he never would.

When her knees would support her again, she returned to the kitchen and opened the card. *Take me back.* A thorn nicked her thumb as she pulled the roses out of the vase and dumped them in the compost bin. She sucked on the wound and descended the stairs back to the basement and her office. She studied the computer screen, then clicked the button. The hum of DNA results printing comforted her.

CHAPTER TWENTY-FIVE

J ahana lay in bed. Last day of Christmas vacation for the girls. She was taking tomorrow off and she had plans. Her fingers hovered over the cell phone. *Where should I meet Barid? At home or in a public place?* Both had their pros and cons. In a public place, his reaction would be more reserved. Always concerned with appearances, he wouldn't want to bring attention to himself but she wanted to see his real reaction and hear his questions. This needed to be over and if they met in a public place, she might not find out everything she wanted. She needed to gauge what he would do next. On the other hand, she worried about his reaction at home. Would he become violent? Her baba's concerns haunted her. Was she being blind to his capabilities? He'd be humiliated and angry, but how would he express it? Being alone with him wasn't an option. Mishal wanted to be there, but Barid never liked Mishal. She would put him on edge the minute he walked in the door. And she didn't want to put Mishal in harm's way either. Her baba was the only person who made sense. But he didn't want her to confront Barid.

She punched out his number.

"Baba, are you okay? So sorry I upset you, can we talk?"

There was a pause before Emad replied. "I'm okay Jahana. Sorry I didn't call you and sorry I walked out of the coffee shop. I'm just worried about you and the girls."

"I understand your concern, but I think confronting Barid with the results is the only way I will get him to leave me alone and let me have custody of the girls. Can you trust me on this?"

Emad cleared his throat and his voice trembled. "You and the girls are all I have. I couldn't bear it if Barid did something to hurt you. Your maman and I raised you to be strong and make your own decisions. While I don't feel like this is the right decision, I will trust you on this one. What alternative is there?"

"Thank you, Baba. I really do think this is the best way to approach Barid. Now, I've decided to meet with him tomorrow. The girls are back in school and I've taken the day off. I'll ask him to come over on his lunch break."

"You're meeting him at your house?" Emad's voice cracked.

"Yes, but I'm hoping you'll be here too. If I meet him in a public place, I'm pretty sure I won't get a true reaction out of him. I won't know what he's thinking. He's so concerned about appearances that it's unlikely he'll say what he really feels. I need to know what he might do. I know you don't agree with my approach, but I need to ask you a favour. Will you be here with me when I reveal my results to him?"

Jahana held her breath.

"I'll be there." His voice filled with resignation.

"If I thought I had any other option, Baba, I wouldn't ask."

****

Her baba arrived early and the two of them sipped tea at the island. Jahana tore at her napkin. There was nothing left inside; her bowels kept her up all night. She glanced at the clock, ten past twelve. The plate of sandwiches sat in front of them. Jahana heard the familiar sound of a code being punched into the door lock followed by the doorbell. Jahana glanced at Emad and made her way to the front door.

"You make me ring my own doorbell? Why'd you change the code on the lock?"

She hadn't acknowledged the roses that appeared when he shouldn't have been able to get in the house, and he hadn't texted her about them.

"I, ah…" Jahana stopped mid-sentence. He almost baited her into clouding the reason he was there. She wouldn't talk about anything other than her results.

Barid brushed past her, his face flushed with irritation. Jahana swallowed. He walked into the kitchen, stopping at the sight of Emad. Emad rose and extended his hand. Barid took it, glancing at Jahana.

"Can I get you some tea?" Jahana pressed the button on the kettle and it set off an instant hum, breaking the awkward silence.

"None for me." Barid grabbed a sandwich, stuffing it into his mouth. Jahana turned off the kettle and settled in beside her baba.

"So why am I here Jahana? Have you changed your mind?" He grabbed another sandwich.

"No. I want to show you my DNA results. Prove I'm not bluffing about having Jewish ancestry." She pushed a manila folder across the island.

Barid looked from the folder to her and back again, then opened it and flipped through the pages. Jahana sat in silence trying to read his stony expression.

He looked across at her. "Did you make this up?"

"Oh Barid. Why would I do that? The results are real. You can see the MyGeneticFamily logo and see I printed it off the website."

Barid studied the documents again. Then looked at Emad.

"Is this true? Were you aware she was Jewish when you adopted her?"

It was just like Barid to seek a male's opinion. Jahana inhaled, grateful her baba was there.

"Yes." Emad looked Barid in the eye, unwavering.

"And you didn't tell me before I married her? What kind of man are you?" Barid slammed his fist on the island. Jahana rose to her feet, knees shaking.

"Barid, Maman and Baba had their reasons. It's complicated. There's nothing we can do about the past, but we can move forward from here."

"Move forward? How will I move forward from this?" Anger hung in the air, but Barid didn't rise continuing to look at the papers in front of him. Jaw muscles working his teeth back and forth.

He looked up, his voice husky and low. "Don't file for divorce. As soon as I get back to the office, I'm setting up an appointment with my lawyer. I'll be the one to file the papers and I don't want anything mentioned to anyone else about this. Is that clear?"

Jahana knees buckled, and she slid back onto the stool before finding her voice. "Okay, I'll wait for the papers. Can we be reasonable about this? No sense paying lawyers any more than necessary." Jahana held her breath, hoping he'd mention the kids.

"Oh, I don't want anything more than my pension investments and my car. I certainly don't want this Jew house." He spat the words out and wiped the back of his hand across his face like he was trying to get rid of a bad taste in his mouth.

Jahana waited patiently.

"Do the girls know they have Jewish blood?"

She could see pain overtake anger in his eyes.

"Yes, I told them two days ago. They're worried about what you'll think."

"Well it'll take some time to figure out how I feel, but I can't see filing for custody."

Jahana let his words land between them. Her body trembled. She didn't trust herself to speak. He reacted the way she thought he would; protect his reputation above all else.

Barid leaned towards her. Emad straightened. Barid grabbed another sandwich off the plate before rising and striding toward the door. It occurred to Jahana he hadn't even taken off his coat. He turned and faced them again, nodding his head at Jahana. "Have you connected with your birth parents?"

"Yes, my mother on the MyGeneticFamily message board. She doesn't know the name of my father."

Barid sneered. "So, you're a bastard too. Should have known."

As if the sandwich had somehow grown tainted, he spit it out and threw the rest on the floor before walking out the front door.

Somehow, he still got the last word.

CHAPTER TWENTY-SIX

An outsider might think Barid won the fight, his words striking the final blow. Jahana stared at the door expecting him to return, laughing, telling her it was all a joke, he'd take the girls from her. A shudder wracked her body, and she leaned on the island for support, knees trembling, bowels cramping, continuing to watch the door. The roar of a car engine told her he was leaving.

The hijab she'd worn to keep him calm and let him think he was still in control, lay in a puddle of black chiffon on the cold tiles, one end still balled in her fist. When had she removed it? Her fist opened and the rest of it floated to the floor. Her baba, watched silently, face ashen.

"Please lock the door."

Barid had driven away, but until the door was locked, she couldn't convince herself he wasn't going to re-appear.

The slide of the deadbolt brought Jahana to her knees. Guttural sobs escaped in jittery gasps.

"Jahni, I'm right here."

His arms surrounded her and her head rested on her baba's shoulder, eyes closed letting a father's love rock her until the sobs subsided.

Barid threw punches with words, but this time was different. She was bruised, not beaten, and the outcome was as good as she could have hoped for. She left the boxing ring with her head held high, with her girls, her house and her freedom. Yet a pit of despair grew. Twenty years of trying to make it work and now the girls wouldn't know what it was like to grow up with a baba in the house.

One deep gasp and she raised her head. Emad released her and wiggled back on his knees, grimacing.

"Oh Baba, I'm so sorry, your knees."

Emad used the stool to pull himself up. "No worries, I'm fine and I'm the one who's sorry. Oh, Jahni, I'm so sorry."

Emad helped Jahana to her feet.

She steadied herself on the island and wiped her nose with a napkin. "Let it go Baba. It happened the way it was meant to. Let it all go."

Emad didn't respond.

Jahana realized the secret no longer bound him, the lie was exposed.

Jahana shuddered again. "So hard to believe he's gone." She faltered and choked back more tears.

"It's okay Jahni, take your time." Emad squeezed her hand.

Her voice cracked, and she paused, taking a deep breath before continuing. "Even though his words controlled me, he was part of my life for a long time and I loved him."

Emad nodded, remaining silent.

"He'll always be the girls' father and he'll always have a piece of my heart. So, there's no need for you to feel guilty about not telling me. This was part of my journey and meant to be."

Jahana forced a weak smile and Emad returned it.

"If you don't mind, Baba, I'd like some time alone to collect myself before the girls come home. Really, I'm okay."

"Are you sure? I can stay."

"I'm sure Baba."

Emad cleaned up the kitchen and the sandwich off the floor before closing the door behind him.

Jahana slid the deadbolt into place and leaned against the door listening to the house. The furnace breathed, the fridge hummed, and the pendulum of the dining room clock ticked rhythmically.

From the living room window, she watched the snow blowing off the roof, swirling, floating down then rising again. *Things work out the way they're supposed to. Barid will no longer define me. Nor will a rapist or a teenage victim. And certainly not my DNA. They don't label me.*

Jahana's resolve strengthened, and she lifted her laptop off the coffee table before settling down on the couch.

As she waited for the MyGeneticFamily account to load, she wondered where living without Barid would take her. How would Barid explain their divorce to his friends and colleagues? A sigh escaped her lips. She reasoned; the people who cared about her would stick by her.

Cyra and Sahba would grow up to be proud of their ancestry and free to make their own choices.

The computer screen sprang to life and she clicked on a new match, expecting to see another distant cousin. Instead the match indicated an extremely likely grandparent, aunt, uncle or half-sibling. There was also a new message. The mouse shook in her hand and she hesitated before clicking on the message from Omar Fassid. She leaned her head back and looked at the ceiling, when would this ever end? She summoned up the courage to read the message.

> *Looks like I may have found a sister! I'm surprised, but then again, not so surprised. My father's always been a bit of a lady's man. Any chance we can communicate and figure this out?*

Her breath caught in her throat. The thing she dreaded the most had happened. Her DNA led her to the son of the man who raped her mother. He had a son. She had a brother. She stared at the screen. This was not something she wanted to consider. He was not someone she wanted to get to know. She closed her laptop and leaned back into the couch once again.

The beeps of a code being punched into the front door brought Jahana back to reality. The deadbolt slid and the front door opened.

"Cyra, give it back!"

Voices echoed down the hall. Jahana set her laptop on the coffee table, rose from the couch and strode to the hall.

"Maman!"

Their voices cushioned her thudding heart.

ABOUT THE AUTHOR

Heather Dawn Gray is a creative writer with a long career in laboratory medicine. After 25 years in healthcare she obtained her Master of Arts in Communications and Technology, formalizing 40 years of dabbling in fiction and non-fiction. Four novel writing courses led by David Allan Hamilton, culminated in the publication of her first novel, a realistic contemporary woman's fiction, 'The Lie'.

Canada is proudly the country Heather identifies as home, but Australia also holds a place in her heart. She has visited several other countries, drawing inspiration from people and places along the way.

It was her own DNA test in 2018 that revealed surprises and led her to question 'What if…' resulting in the birth of her first fiction novel, 'The Lie' and its sequel 'Where Truth Lies'.

Heather currently resides in Ottawa Ontario Canada with her soulmate, Ron. They have two daughters, Sabra and Colby, who are pursuing their professional careers in Alberta Canada and Queensland Australia.

Visit her webpage at https://heatherdawngray.com/

Made in the USA
Coppell, TX
20 February 2021